BESOTTED

A NOVEL
BY MELISSA DUCLOS

7.13 BOOKS

BROOKLYN, NY

"*Besotted* is an absorbing, nuanced debut about belonging, desire, and the frustrations that surface in an atmosphere of isolation. Set mostly in tiny apartments, ridiculous happy hour bars, and Starbucks—all Western attempts to recreate home—Duclos's expatriate Shanghai is wholly unique and beautifully composed. Alive with keenly observed, vibrant detail, Besotted is a love story that pulses with heat and light, glitter and grit."
Kimberly King Parsons, author of *Black Light*

"In *Besotted*, Melissa Duclos debuts a beautiful, bruising love story that fully inhabits the world's disquieting spaces in between. Her tender, vital community of Shanghai expats are—sometimes in the space of a single, lyric sentence—both impulsive and calculating, passionate and standoffish, at home and as far from home as they possibly can be. The result is an exuberant, sexy tango of a novel, at turns playful and wrenching, that unpacks the ways desire and reality are both closer together and farther apart than they ever initially seem."
Tracy Manaster, *author of The Done Thing*

"*Besotted* is an exquisite tale of desire, longing, love, and reinvention. Duclos's brilliance lies in her painstaking renderings of heartaches large and small, and the particular pain of struggling to find connection on the other side of the world. Besotted is a head rush—a sexier, smarter, more genuine coming-of-age story you will not find."
Mo Daviau, *author of Every Anxious Wave*

"The true star of this piece is the expat community that Duclos has perfectly drawn. Any expat who has spent an amount of time in Asia will find at least something in there that speaks to their own experience. The worldbuilding is excellent."
Kirkus Reviews

"Readers of *Besotted* should be alert as Melissa Duclos slips in and out of the different points of view, jump cutting from one consciousness to the next with boldness and precision; her snarky slings land on target and slice deep. This novel about what country, friendship, work, and above all love mean to a generation of American expats also touches on what life in China is like for its cosmopolitan masses. But Loneliness, capitalized by Duclos, is the main theme. The clueless characters of *Besotted* try to hide their vulnerabilities under layers of coolness, clever remarks, and disaffection. They are very much like the people we know; they are us at the end of the day, when we remove our makeup and can't any longer disguise how much love and the lack of it can hurt."
Jaime Manrique, author of *Cervantes Street*

"In this Jamesian comedy of manners, Melissa Duclos chronicles—with sharp intelligence and an insider's knowledge—Shanghai's elite expat community, to devastating, transfixing effect."
Joanna Rakoff, author of *My Salinger Year*

Printed and distributed by 7.13 Books. First paper-
back edition, first printing: March 2019

Cover design: Gigi Little
Author photo: Katherine Duclos

ISBN-10: 1-7328686-4-6
ISBN-13: 978-1-7328686-4-9

Library of Congress Control Number: 2018962337

For Teddy and Ellie.
You know my heart.

But all attractions are alike...They come from an emptiness inside...Something's missing and you have to fill it.

Distortion is part of desire. We always change the things we want.

—Siri Hustvedt, *The Blindfold*

WHAT I HAVE LEFT

璸

SUCH A THING IS POSSIBLE

爱

WE WISH FOR STARS

氛

WE STAND WITHOUT MOVING

照片

SAYING THINGS ALOUD MAKES THEM TRUE

家

WHAT I HAVE LEFT

瓃

I once considered the space that exists between what people say and what they mean to be my native habitat. Until Liz. None of my adaptations or manipulations helped me understand her. I remained a foreigner in that space. Just another *lǎowài* in Shanghai.

Last year, during my search for an apartment that could be a home for us—one with a private entrance off a courtyard, a southern-facing bedroom and sliding glass door into the garden, dark wood fretwork behind the couch, a full-sized oven—she told me that all empty apartments look the same. It took me too long to realize what she meant: look all you want, Bunny Rabbit. I won't be living in any of them.

The emptying of my current apartment—the one I found for Liz but moved into alone—happened gradually. The couch where we kissed sold first, followed by the dishes (minus the ones she'd chipped), the bed we shared, the lamp with the hand-painted red silk shade that she hated. Each day I felt a steady hand slicing away at my life, the way a surgeon might remove tumors. Or, this is just how I've been feeling for the last year.

What I have left of my four years in Shanghai is either depressing or virtuous. Either way I'll be arriving in Berlin tomorrow with two suitcases full of clothes and a cashier's check for ¥38,457.84, that will become €4,491.42. I'm 26 years old, and this is all I have in the world.

That's not entirely true. All I have are two suitcases full of clothes and a wooden box I can't bring myself to open. I could have dropped it in the dumpster at the end of the driveway; hidden it in the mondo grass in the courtyard; taken it out onto the lanai, lit it on fire, and encircled it in Chinese fireworks that would scare whatever ghosts emanated from its ashes. I came very close to leaving it in the back of the dresser, imagining the new owners piecing together my relationship with Liz from its detritus—movie stubs and a strip of photos spit out by a booth in Xiujiahua, the cryptic sticky notes we used to leave on each other's desks, the blank green envelopes I never got around to using, the letters, from Liz and from the school—but the English banker who bought the dresser didn't seem to have an imagination worthy of it, so I changed my mind.

I should've thrown it away after she left, but I don't often do what I should. And so now I have a box best suited to carry ashes or medals from war. Its lid is carved with the image of two birds, facing and circling each other around a branch of plum blossoms. I used to love it.

I imagine shoving the box into my suitcase—a checked bag I'll pretend to hope gets lost from Shanghai to Abu Dhabi to Belgrade to Berlin. But I know I can't pack it away without opening it.

I crack the lid and close my eyes, and the first thing I feel isn't a sticky note or a glossy photo. It's pearl—single strand. I don't need to bring the necklace to my teeth to know it's real. I've tasted it before.

1.

There are 15 international schools in Shanghai catering to the children of wealthy expatriates, businessmen, and their families, from Asia, Europe, America—all of them wielding the requisite foreign passports and paying the thousands of dollars in tuition. Like their students, the teachers come from all over the world, though only the Chinese instructors are from China. Native English is required, and in some schools a British or Australian accent will get you further than teaching experience. Most new teachers work in language institutes—night schools for adults—but the lucky ones find places at the international schools that provide work visas, housing, and transportation. Liz never understood that she was lucky, and she didn't know why I'd hired her.

She was Elizabeth to me then: an English major two years out of college who spoke no Chinese and had no teaching experience but who'd been hired anyway because I was lonely. I'd been living in Shanghai for three years, shouldn't have had to import new friends from America.

But there was my spare bedroom, empty for the previous year; there was the suffocating quiet.

I knew what it meant when Loneliness moved in. Loneliness took up all available space, breathed the air meant for me, absorbed the heat and left me shivering. Pretending to enjoy Loneliness's company didn't help; she was immune to reverse psychology. Loneliness needed to be driven out by loud laughter and unpredictable comings and goings. There were already countless loud and entitled Americans in Shanghai, but what did they want from me? Liz would need my help, I knew, to navigate the city and succeed at her job. "You're moving out soon," I said aloud to Loneliness, projecting confidence I didn't remotely feel. I didn't know what else to do.

It took a long time for me to ask Liz why she moved to Shanghai, and though I'm pretty sure she was honest with me, I'm not sure what she said was the truth. I'm not sure she was capable of that. At the time, I didn't wonder what she wanted from the move; I was too wrapped up in what I wanted from her.

She must have thought of her life as just beginning when she arrived here, as though she were throwing open a door that had been closed for years. She was the type of person who thought in terms of transformations and opportunities waiting to be seized.

September in Shanghai, though, is not a time for new beginnings, no matter what the school calendar says. The air here the night Liz arrived was soft and suffocating like tufted felt, the heat from the day still radiating, grimy and moist, from the concrete, glass, and tile of the city.

There is nothing new about September here, except for the construction projects that know no season dotting the city, but the Liz in my memory saw what she wanted to see. From the backseat of her van, as it hurtled away from the airport, under the Huangpu River, through Old Town and out the other side, she imagined her future written out in neon lights. The skyscrapers were at first too close to the side of the highway for her to really see them, and so she watched the guardrails, flashing purple, blue, and green, implying speed and glamour.

She compared this to her arrival in New York City, two years prior, when she'd been one of the thousands of college graduates to arrive in Brooklyn, feeling as though she accomplished something simply by moving out of her parents' house, even though it was her father who sweated and swore his way up three flights of stairs with her futon, her dresser, her boxes of books.

The van stopped in front of her hotel and Liz got out, and after a moment of waiting for the driver to help with the bags, she hauled them from the trunk herself, offered a polite nod, and approached the door. The glass slid aside automatically in front of her, making a sound like a sword slicing through the air. She stepped into the empty lobby, listening to the echo of her footsteps, and adjusted her posture, trying to appear as though she did this sort of thing—this arriving-in-a-foreign-country-knowing-no-one-not-even-speaking-the-language sort of thing—every day. At the front desk she slid her passport to the slight woman who appeared from a door in the corner, checking into the room the school had provided without saying a word. She dragged her bags toward the elevator.

The hotel room was not exactly nice, but it was close enough. She didn't know whether to unpack or not, unsure whether this hotel room—with no kitchen, no separate living area—constituted the "lodgings" Principal Wu had mentioned in his e-mail. So she put roughly half her clothes into the small dresser, choosing them arbitrarily, and as she did, noticed a glossy green envelope lying on the dresser top. I know because I put it there.

Of some parts of this story I'm certain.

Inside the envelope was a matching green piece of paper, folded in half. On the front: *The size of the steps is not important, as long as they are going in the right direction.*

It was hard for Liz not to feel the card was a coded message. She looked around the room, suddenly feeling as though she were being watched. I'm going in the right direction, she wanted to shout. The note felt like an indictment, a passive aggressive judgment of the kind her mother would deliver. She looked at it again and only then thought to open it.

Meet your driver outside the hotel at 7:00 a.m.

That was all. Liz sighed and shook her head, settling down onto the bed. It was just a note from the school after all. A bizarre one, but just a note. She had so many questions—about when her training would begin and where she would really be living—but as she turned the piece of paper over in hand, it became clear none of them would be answered tonight. Seven in the morning would come quickly, she knew, and so she fought through nerves and jetlag and forced herself to go to bed. As she lay skirting the edges of unconsciousness, she thought of Bryan and wished he could have seen her there.

Right on time the next morning, Liz's van sped along the highway away from the city, confusing her. She'd assumed without checking that the school was downtown. But they drove and drove, leaving the highway for dusty side streets lined with factories: Shanghai Lightbulb #7, and the like. Finally, after an hour's drive, they pulled into the gate behind a line of five yellow school busses. She glanced out the back window as they came to a stop and saw two more busses making the turn behind them. Children streamed off in orderly lines, moving quickly through the wide double doors at the front of the school.

For a long time I carried an image of Liz in the back of

the van on that morning, nervously fingering her necklace and chewing on her lower lip, sitting frozen in the back seat until the driver turned and waved his hand at her, as though shooing away a fly. But maybe that's not how she was.

Once she entered the school, I watched her from behind my desk, separated from her by the narrow main hallway and a wall of plate glass windows at the front of my office. The main office, really, but I always thought of it as mine. It was always so sunny.

She wore a dark brown pencil skirt that was too heavy for the season and too formal for our school, a crisp peach blouse. She had nice shoes on—teacher shoes—brown with a modest heel, and slender ankles. I thought she needed to gain 10 pounds, not out of any jealousy for her thin frame, but because she looked to need some kind of cushioning from the rest of the world, as though perhaps the angles of her knees, hips, and elbows were a danger to her. She was sharp where she needed curves, with straight, shoulder-length hair pinned back from her face. She was taller than I expected she'd be, and from the look of her slightly hunched shoulders, taller than she expected herself to be, too.

I knew she didn't know where to go, or what was expected of her. I could've gone out immediately to greet her, just as I could've left a more informative letter in her hotel room. But I let her stand there alone, wanting—perhaps cruelly—for this woman to feel a moment of terror at life here without any help. I was cruel, right from the start; there's no use trying to hide that.

2.

I knew so many things Liz didn't. I knew the silver van would take her to and from school each day, directly back to her hotel and nowhere else, and that to get into the city she'd have to call a cab, in Chinese. I knew finding an apartment required luck and connections the school had no official plans to provide; I knew she'd have to register as a foreign visitor with the local police department and pay her electric bill at the convenience store. No one else would tell Liz these things, because telling her was my job. I looked at this new teacher, her pearl necklace glinting in the sunlight, surrounded by new colleagues who had not made eye contact and did not want to be her friend.

"You must be Elizabeth," I came out from behind my desk finally with my hand extended.

"Liz," she corrected. She didn't look scared.

"Principal Wu will be ready for you in just a minute. I'm his assistant, Sasha. Have a seat," I gestured toward a couch on the other side of the room. "Can I get you some water?"

I was trying my best to appear disinterested. I handed her the water, smiled as she retreated to the couch, and then returned to my desk, pretending to work. It was the best I could do. To actually begin work on the database of student names and addresses I needed to finish was unthinkable. Instead, I stared past my computer screen, studying the woman who sat a few feet away.

When the principal finally called her into his office, she stood and took a deep breath, looking relieved. I nodded my head as she passed.

Principal Wu closed his door and I turned back to my desk, looking blankly at the stack of student registration forms I was to enter into the school's database. The letters blurred together, though, and so I closed my eyes, wishing them out of existence.

At that point I'd been living alone for a year. It wasn't by choice, but a couple of weeks after Joanne moved out, I'd convinced myself that it was a good idea. The solitude would be refreshing, I thought. *Rejuvenating! Reinvigorating!!* I punctuated each new adjective with more exclamations than the last, and though the inside of my head was starting to sound like some kind of insane shampoo commercial on an endless loop, I didn't stop. Couldn't stop. Feigned happiness, I thought, would be an effective deterrent to Loneliness.

Except it wasn't.

After a couple of months I felt lied to, though the lies had all been my own. I saw in Liz a chance to make things better.

She was looking to make things better, too. Even before I knew her I realized that. People who don't speak Chinese, who don't have any teaching experience, don't suddenly decide to move to Shanghai on a whim. People like that are usually running from something, and though her application revealed no deep sadness, I assumed. I was running from sadness, too.

The beginning was the hardest. I had to let her flounder a bit, but I lived with the anxiety that it would be too much for her to handle, that those first few days of uncertainty would be enough to send her home. But I needed to see what she was made of.

Principal Wu started with his standard speech. "We're so happy to have another American representative at our school," he said softly, after Liz had taken a seat in front of his desk, as though she were an American emissary sent to The Singapore School of Shanghai.

"I'm happy to be here," she answered, because she was here and was indeed happy and eventually would have to stop wondering how it had all happened.

"We will need you to be flexible about your timetable. There have been some changes."

The contract the school had sent had been vague. She had visions of high schoolers discussing *A Separate Peace* or *Brave New World*, answering her provocative questions in eloquent essays. But she would take any assignment. She assured him she could be very flexible.

"Which musical instruments can you play?"

This question confused her. "None."

"Only the piano?"

"No, not the piano. I can't play any instruments." No amount of flexibility would turn her into a music teacher. She wondered then whether there'd been some mistake. Somewhere in New York there was a music teacher with an impressive résumé waiting for her plane ticket. She wondered how long it would be before she was sent back to America. For just a moment she prayed it would happen quickly.

She tried to stay calm, though. She continued to bluff. "I was an English major. I was hired to teach English."

"Yes," he agreed, shuffling through a stack of papers, seemingly looking for something. Then he repeated: "But as I said, the school requires some flexibility. There have been changes in your timetable." He explained that she wouldn't be teaching a regular English class. The school needed her, instead, to teach four sections of first-grade speech.

"Parents have been unhappy with the class."

"What's speech class? And what does that have to do with playing instruments?"

"Speech is talking," he said, as though that explained anything. At Liz's furrowed brow he continued. "Modeling a proper accent and grammar. It is usually taught with singing."

"Do I have to teach it that way?"

"No," he answered slowly. "But that's the way it's usually done."

There was a long pause, as Liz considered her response. Principal Wu, a nervous man who avoided conflict at all costs, broke the silence first.

"However, I respect the experience you bring to the position. If you have another approach, I'm sure it will be a great success."

Liz brought no experience at all, which is one of the reasons she was my first choice, but Principal Wu didn't know that. I was counting on her, though, to realize she wasn't qualified; the job was a gift I wanted her to be grateful for.

After their brief conversation, Principal Wu took Liz upstairs to the staffroom, handed her a stack of papers—the orientation packet I'd assembled for her—and pointed her toward her desk, set in a cluster with the four other first grade teachers. He hurried away then, waving his hands at the rest of the teachers, or perhaps holding them protectively in front of his face.

The women seated around Liz each had their own

classrooms, their own groups of students, to whom they taught reading, math, and history. Liz would appear in each of their rooms for one period a day to talk with the children.

They glared at her. They didn't speak directly to her, but they talked loudly about a woman named Felisha and the food she used to bring them.

"Remember the almond biscuits?" one of them said while Liz looked through the drawers of her new desk.

"The toffee apples?"

"The durian cakes?"

Over the course of that first day Liz learned that Felisha, the teacher parents had complained about, had been fired two months ago and sent back to Singapore, that she had a troublesome son, that her husband was always away on business. All of these things were somehow Liz's fault.

At that moment, sitting at her desk, she began to look through the packet of PowerPoint slides titled "The English Teacher," understanding finally that they constituted the only training she would receive. On the front was an illustration of a young white woman, smiling in front of a room of Asian children. Liz opened the packet, expecting to find helpful information about what she should be teaching, or how, but instead found more illustrations: a picture of the young woman reading a newspaper at her desk, while the children in the class stood around the room, their arms extended in the air. That one had a big X beneath it. On the next page the young woman was standing at the front of the room, pointing at the word HELLO written on the board. The children sat at their desks, their hands folded in front of them. That picture had a large check mark beneath it.

The whole packet was like this: a big X for letting students attempt to climb out the window, approach the blackboard, or punch each other in the face. Check marks for arranging them in groups, for hanging their work on the wall and gesturing toward it, smiling. If it were me I would have laughed—did laugh, in fact, while I was putting the packet together. I don't know if Liz laughed, though. She didn't cry. I would've heard about that. And she didn't quit.

Beneath the packet, sandwiched between a form with instructions for picking up her pay and another listing school holidays and closures, she saw a green envelope, the same glossy paper she'd found in her hotel room. She waited until it seemed the other teachers were occupied with their own papers and plans, and then quietly opened it. Inside she found the same folded piece of green paper. This time, the message on the front read: *A tiger doesn't lose sleep over the opinion of sheep.*

Liz didn't understand. Was the woman in all the pictures, pushing her students' desks together and preventing them from falling out of windows, a tiger or a sheep? The other teachers in the staff room, none of whom had greeted her and who all sat now with their heads down at their desks certainly seemed like sheep, but how was Liz supposed to be a tiger and still do what was required of her? She sighed and opened the note, hoping for some kind of explanation.

She read: Please provide the office staff with your new address by the end of the week. She read the note over a second time, then a third, wondering if words like "provide" and "end of the week" might perhaps mean something different in Shanghai. She tucked the envelope inside her desk, trying to ignore her rising panic.

She wasn't expecting to have to teach on her first day, and yet there she was, later that afternoon, standing outside Ms. Rose's classroom, waiting to carry on a 45-minute conversation with 22 seven-year-olds, armed with a list of questions that sounded more like openers for a blind date. She'd spent that morning looking through the English textbooks her students were using.

"You can't teach them that. We are teaching them that," one of the teachers had snapped at her.

"I just want to see, so I know what to do in speech class."

"Speech is talking. You talk in speech class."

You talk in speech class, Liz whispered under her breath as she peered into the classroom. She wanted to run but had nowhere to go. Then the door opened and she went in.

"Hello, class. I'm your new speech teacher," here she paused; she didn't know how to refer to herself. "Elizabeth." It was default more than decision. She waited a moment and five hands shot up into the air.

"Yes?" She pointed at a little girl in the front row.

"Where is Ms. Felisha?"

Calling on the first student opened the door; once she began answering their questions she didn't know how to stop. She spent more than half the class explaining that Ms. Felisha had gone back to Singapore, that she herself had moved from New York, was 24 years old, didn't live with her parents, didn't have a boyfriend, did like Shanghai, didn't know how to speak Chinese, had never been to Korea, Japan, Taiwan, Hong Kong, or Singapore—places she assumed each of the askers had come from—but that she was interested in trying foods from all those places. After a while students stopped raising their hands and began instead to shout out their questions as they thought of them.

She didn't know how to control them. For a time she thought she owed them these answers; she was, after all, a stranger in their class, not to be trusted, in need of testing. When they asked her why she'd come to China, why she was a teacher, she began to feel exposed. She didn't have answers that seven-year-olds would understand. So she lied.

"I've been a teacher for three years," she told them. "In America. I've always wanted to live in China, though, so I transferred here." Transfer sounded to her like a more official word than moved. The children nodded their heads, perhaps confused, or finally out of questions. Liz seized the opportunity. "Now I'd like you to tell me about yourselves. We'll go around the room and you'll tell me your name and what country you're from."

As she pointed to a child sitting in the front row, she saw an unfamiliar teacher standing just inside the door in the back of the room.

"It's time for art class," he said when he caught Liz's eye.

The children cheered and stood up, quickly forming a line at the back of the classroom. Liz forced a smile. How long had he been standing there, she wondered, listening to her talk about herself and teach her students nothing? She felt her face redden as she followed the line of children and their art teacher out of the class, hoping her failure wouldn't be reported to anyone who mattered.

3.

When Liz left Shanghai I felt robbed. At the same time I hated the fact of that metaphor. I yearned for the tangible and concrete—something I could have shown to the police. My heart, my lungs, the taste I used to awaken with every morning on my tongue. They've all been taken, I might have said.

She had accomplices. Dorian, a typical architect, delusional in his belief that he could shape the world to his liking, had imagined a different ending, and I could never explain to him how wrong he was. He thought I was just like him, that I loved Shanghai. But to me it's always been just a hiding place.

The city looks like the set of a science fiction movie: the concrete and steel towers, all looming too close to the sidewalks, lit from below to make them seem more imposing; the eight-lane highways, congested with cars creeping ever forward, their headlights refracted in the thick smog; the four-story neon Chinese characters marking the restaurants, the supermarkets, the banks. It wasn't difficult to imagine retinal scanners on the traffic lights, processing the throngs of people—three rows deep in some of the more popular shopping districts—waiting to cross the street. And then there were the soldiers, erect in their brown uniforms, crisp and dry despite the heat of the morning, drilling in the square in front of McDonald's, preparing for a future no one wanted to think about. They did it silently, which was perhaps the strangest part. No "hup, hup, hup" and even the click of their boots somehow muffled. Dorian and I paid them no mind, though. At least not by that year.

We understood the bureaucracy. We registered with the local police station when we first arrived, as all foreigners were required. We underwent the labyrinthine series of medical examinations necessary to receive our work visas. The policeman Dorian sat across from in the medical offices, after the third test of his liver function was deemed "too high" refused to look him in the eye. He negotiated, instead, with the office manager of Dorian's firm, a slight Chinese man with a lisp. Eventually, a fee was settled upon, the visa issued. There was no discussion about a follow-up with the doctor, or what, if anything, Dorian needed to do for his liver. It was a shakedown, his colleagues told him later. I agreed. There's nothing wrong with his liver, and we bought him many 20-ounce bottles of Tsingtao to prove it. Welcome to China.

That was all a few years before Liz had arrived. By the time she showed up, Dorian had changed. Shanghai was a city always looking toward the future, and three years after Dorian showed up, so was he. The few friends he'd told thought he was crazy for wanting to buy in China. They weren't bad friends, but they were expats. Expats don't own furniture, never mind the apartments or houses in which to put it. They arrive with dingy frame backpacks, or heavy suitcases on wheels, which they learn to pack and unpack quickly. They crash on each other's couches, or each other's floors, and even when they do find their own apartments, they live as though still crashing. They buy one mug, one bowl, one set of chopsticks. They debate the need for a shower curtain.

Expats are temporary people, seeking temporary lives. But Dorian wanted permanence. In a different life, he and I might have made a good match, his constancy a good counter-balance to my self-destructive impulsivity.

He walked to work, cutting through Xintiandi. The renovation of the old French Quarter, its name meaning "New Heaven and Earth," was completed the previous year. The American architect scrapped plans to tear down the nineteenth century Shikumen-style buildings in favor of skyscrapers. He kept the old instead, preserving façades and repurposing the buildings to house high-end restaurants and boutiques. There's also a mall.

Dorian would've preferred the skyscrapers. The past, he believed, wasn't necessarily worth preserving just because it was old. The city's developers seemed to agree, more often employing bulldozers than chisels in their quest to re-globalize the city, turning it back into the cultural and financial hub that it was in the 1930s. The architecture of the city then—in the French Concession, along the Bund—was distinct. There was nothing distinctive, in Dorian's opinion, in the restoration of old façades; they looked more to him like Walt Disney's idea of China. While many of his expat friends treated Shanghai like their own personal Neverland, Dorian saw more in the city's future than that.

He liked the metaphor and thought of the laughs it would get at happy hour. It was Zapata's that night. It was hard to know how things like that were decided, who made the call. It wasn't as though there was some kind of Expat Happy Hour committee choosing the bar. But he got the group text each week, just like I did. Just like anyone who'd moved here and met another expat. Of course, not all of them showed up. It's hard to say how many expatriates live here. Does a migrant worker from the Philippines count? Or just the well-educated Europeans, Americans, Australians—the ones who stand in line at the consulates, apply for their visas, get jobs at English schools and foreign companies? Two hundred thousand, then, or maybe four. The community seemed much smaller than that though. If we counted only the ones we saw regularly—the ones who got the group texts and came to happy hours after work, went to the clubs on weekends—it was maybe just 40 or 50 people.

Dorian always wondered where the rest of them went, how the community the size of a modest city could end up feeling as small as a college fraternity. The rest of them, he assumed, were real people, out living real lives: jobs and families and houses and grocery shopping, all of it just happening to take place in China. Not like the expats he knew, mostly working for beer and travel money. It didn't stop Dorian from going to the happy hours, getting drunk with some of them, sleeping with others. He was done with that, though. It was time to grow up.

4.

Liz and I made it to that happy hour, but the first week of school leading up to it was a trial. My certainty that Liz's insecurities at work would drive her to confide in me wavered. It would take time and time and time, I told myself. Everything takes time, but there were afternoons that week, long afternoons when the sunlight slanted through the glass-paned front doors of the school, when I would hold my breath and pretend that it was all done already: Loneliness driven out, the empty caverns within me no longer gaping, gasping. But nothing was done. Nothing had changed. The silence still cut into me, leaving tracks.

Just ask her, I would growl inside my own head, or occasionally out loud, when the office was filled with the cacophony of teachers and all their silly problems and I felt sure that my own complaints, offered to myself and the universe, would be lost. Just ask her to move in. But I couldn't. It's hard for me to understand now what scared me so much. My memories are crowded by my knowledge of how things turned out, the way you can never quite remember the feeling of being lost after you have come to know a place.

Whatever the cause of my fear, I didn't push past it. Instead, I watched Liz shuffle the hallways and made sure to seem in a terrible rush whenever we passed. I knew when she ate lunch—knew her whole timetable by heart, in fact—and on Thursday of the first week of school, I finally sat down at one of the empty stools at her usual table.

"I'm sorry I haven't had time to come and eat with you sooner," I hurried, hoping with speed to project importance. "It's just, you know the beginning of the school year is so busy for me."

Liz nodded, gulping down the bite of eggplant she'd been chewing. "That's okay. I mean, it's not your job—"

"Oh, of course it's not my job," I cut her off. "But still, I know how lonely this place can be."

She didn't respond, and I understood, knowing that to acknowledge Loneliness was to invite her to stay. I didn't push, and instead made small talk while we ate our steamed pork buns and eggplant over rice. I pointed subtly to the other teachers around the cafeteria, telling Liz which one had almost been fired over the summer, which one spent weekends with the principal and his family, which one had once slapped a student.

"So a bunch of us are going out tomorrow night. You should come," I mentioned casually as we were finishing up. A bunch.

"I would love that," she answered quickly, without waiting for any further details. "Oh, but how will I get there? I just get dropped off at that horrible hotel every day. I don't know if I can get a cab."

"Just come home with me tomorrow after school," I offered. "You can crash at my place and go back to the hotel on Saturday." I was careful about the offer, knowing not to suggest too much, too soon.

"That sounds amazing. Thank you."

I shrugged. "No big deal." I stood abruptly, taking my tray in my hands. "Bring something fun to wear." I hurried away from the table, knowing I probably seemed rude. I was afraid, though, that if I lingered I wouldn't be able to stop myself from pleading with her: Come and stay and stay and stay.

Liz left the hotel on Friday morning with a small bag of clothes.

"Checking out?" the woman at the desk called as she hurried by to meet her van outside.

She stopped, surprised. The hotel staff had never spoken to her before, and she wasn't aware that they knew English. "Oh, um, no, not yet." She thought of the green envelope she'd received earlier in the week; the deadline for providing the school with her new address was today.

"Are you sure?" the woman spoke loudly from behind the desk.

Liz hovered by the door, feeling somehow that as long as she didn't cross the lobby, the woman had no power. "Yes." Her voice projected confidence. "Yes, I'm sure."

The woman furrowed her brow and looked down at a sheet of paper, seeming to calculate something. Liz took the opportunity to flee through the revolving door, out into the heat of the morning to meet her driver.

She should have come to me for help. She hurried to the staff room instead, stashing her small bag under her desk lest anyone else see it and mistake this for moving day. Later that afternoon she saw the principal coming down the hallway and she hid in the women's bathroom. She didn't think about it; she simply ducked inside, as though the school couldn't evict her if they couldn't find her. In the stall she got angry—that the school expected her to find her own apartment. We would've provided one for her, though, if she'd asked.

Meanwhile, the green envelopes were piling up. I'd put another one atop a pile of announcements at her first staff meeting on Wednesday. She'd opened it and read the quote on the front: *Great change may not happen right away, but with effort even the difficult may become easy.* She'd looked around the room, wondering if everyone received the same messages; they all seemed particularly relevant to her life. She'd been nervous to open the note, wondering what new and impossible task she'd be given, but the card was blank inside. I just wanted to encourage her to keep trying.

On Thursday I'd put another one in her mailbox. *To know but not to do is not to know at all.* Inside, the note instructed her to turn in all her lesson plans by the end of next week, making two looming deadlines.

I wasn't making them up. That seems important to get straight. There's a difference between lying and arranging the truth.

I don't know what she did with the notes. I was expecting her to mention them when she got to my apartment. I see you have an extra bedroom, she might have said. But something held her back. She watched me puttering around, finishing getting ready, and something must have made her nervous.

I recognized it. I'd been registering the sideways glances since junior high. The eyes, slightly wide, always indicated envy, but the pursed lips spoke of disapproval. There was something about me that other women found threatening, but at the same time wanted to possess. I still don't understand what it is: round breasts, maybe, but those are common; the thick, dark hair that hung down my back in loose waves, perhaps; my pale skin, or almond-shaped eyes. Or it's the combination; like a poisonous frog in the jungle, I am somehow marked as dangerous. I'd worked hard to fight against this impression, but finally, in the long years before Liz arrived in China, I'd come to understand the ways in which kindness can be read as desperation.

I was trying a new approach with Liz, walking a new line.

"Do I look okay?" she asked me.

Instead of nodding enthusiastically as would've been my nature, I tipped my head to one side, studying her for a moment until I could see she was uncomfortable. "I have a better shirt for you," I told her. "Hold on."

She looked relieved, which told me everything.

I dawdled getting ready, offering her a beer, giving her time to ask me about the green envelopes, the missed deadlines that must have been weighing on her. I had my response all prepared: a sympathetic nod, and then the flash of inspiration in my eyes, the surprised realization that Liz could just move in with me. "I have this extra room," I'd laugh, as though it had just appeared in front of us, the shimmering answer to her problem. She said nothing, though, and I began to wonder if she had more resources than I thought, if she'd solved the problem on her own.

This was all just typical Liz. She was incapable of direct conversation. That night, before I understood this, I felt anxious. When we got in the cab, I already knew how drunk I would get. I could feel it coming, like a storm.

5.

Expats love happy hour. It's a particularly American concept, but the Chinese understand its value and have packaged it well for the *lǎowài*. The bars tend to offer their deals for foreigners haphazardly—one week Glamour Bar might offer a 10 percent discount on martinis, another night it's all you can drink at Mural. Expats love a good deal of course, but more than that they love to be in the know, an affliction of those who willingly settle in a place where they will always be viewed as outsiders. Getting invitations to all the right happy hours meant something, then.

That week Zapata's was offering two-for-one 16-ounce frozen margaritas from six to nine. After that anyone left still ordering them was too drunk to care that they cost an outrageous ¥90. Happy hour was more crowded than usual when we arrived, even though Zapata's was one of the bigger bars in the rotation. People stood two rows deep along the heavy oak bar that ran the length of the restaurant; on the other side every table was full, and the ones on the patio were as well, though few people were actually sitting, preferring instead to stand and mingle.

We inched our way through the crowd, each of us looking to drown our own butterflies. I ordered our margaritas—in English, from a German bartender—and turned to face the throng of almost entirely white faces. The few Chinese who came to bars like this for happy hours paid more for their drinks than we did, for the privilege of standing amidst the international patrons.

"It's busier because school just started," I leaned in close to explain to Liz. The English teachers had returned. They traveled over the summer, or they went home having completed their grand adventures, to be replaced in the fall by a new batch of wide-eyed Americans and Europeans, all waving their TOEFL certifications proudly. They were like an incoming crop of freshmen on a college campus, or, perhaps more accurately, a new bunch of summer camp counselors: entirely replaceable, possessing next to no actual expertise they could apply to their jobs, all of them merely in it for the experience. I often wondered what these people would do if they didn't move to China: they'd be waiters, perhaps, or work in bookstores, Banana Republic, until they grew up and went to grad school.

Liz was probably the least qualified among them that night. Before I really knew her, I assumed she realized that.

Dorian was there, standing at the other end of the bar, glowering at the crowd in front of him, a half-drunk beer in his hand. He downed the rest of it. I expected to see him turn toward the door, but instead he signaled to the bartender for another. He was the only person there not drinking a margarita. This was typical of him. "I like to keep my wits about me," he used to say. But that night he wasn't smiling.

He was handsome. That wasn't my opinion, but rather an objective fact. His jaw was square, and his dark hair, cut short on the sides but left long on top, accentuated the angles of his face. His features were in perfect proportion, his mouth a square under the isosceles triangle of his nose.

His eyes were always bluer than I expected them to be. He was from Portland, and the first night we really talked, after seeing each other out at the bars for a few months, I asked him something about life on the West Coast. Maybe I'd told him I had ideas about going there "next." Expats often talk like that, listing cities they plan to move to the way normal people discuss the movies they'd like to see.

I don't remember the rest of our conversation. I remember the dark corner of Glamour Bar. Dorian stood facing me, leaning forward onto his hand, which rested on the wall behind my head. He is nearly eight inches taller, and I must have been wearing flats that night because I remember craning my neck to look up at him. He is slender, but very muscular, not at all awkward. I remember the tendons in his wrist, the slight bulge of the muscle in his forearm, the triangle of freckles on his wrist, pointing like an arrow to the bottom of a tattoo that peeked out from the cuff of his rolled-up sleeve.

With his other hand he plucked at a few strands of my hair, bringing them close to his face as he spoke, as though examining them for some secret. I don't think he knew how nervous he made me. I finished my vodka with Red Bull so fast the ice had not begun to melt. My hand grew cold, but I had nowhere to set the glass down.

He didn't try to kiss me. I've wondered many times over the past few months how things might have been different if he'd just done it then. But he was interrupted, and he stood up straight, took his hand off the wall.

That was all. The next time I saw him out, he was standing in the exact same position with a tallish blonde girl I'd never seen before. It seemed after that night that he was always standing in a dark corner with some blonde girl who'd only just arrived in the country. It didn't take me long to figure out what Dorian was all about. He didn't date Chinese women, like the other Western men, but he was just the same as them anyway. We became friends, if only because we both stayed put while everyone else around us came and went.

I watched him scanning the room until his eyes settled on me and Liz. He wove his way toward us, his full beer just above his shoulder to keep it safe from the crowds.

"So you're the new one?"

Liz started at the touch on her elbow, and it took a moment for her to realize that Dorian was talking to her. If nothing else, he was predictable.

"Dorian! Slumming it with the plebes tonight?"

He raised his hands in mock surrender. "I do try to make time for the little people. Who's your friend?" He turned to Liz before I had a chance to answer. "Let me guess: you got here…last week?"

Who could blame me for assuming he was flirting with her? And who could blame me for panicking? If there was anyone else who'd be able to help solve the problems I was causing Liz at work, it was Dorian.

She introduced herself and offered her hand as she swallowed a sip of her drink. "And yes, it's been a week. Do I still look jetlagged?"

"No, you're fine. I just know Sasha always does such a good job taking care of the newcomers."

"I was about to say the same of you," I interjected quietly. Liz didn't hear me, but I'm sure Dorian did.

"She's been a lifesaver, actually. I'm staying at her place tonight."

"Liz works at the school with me," I explained quickly.

"Naturally. What else would she do?" Dorian grinned and took a long sip off his beer, his eyes fixed on Liz.

"Just ignore him. Dorian thinks that foreign architects and lawyers have more of a right to Shanghai than English teachers do."

"Not true. I hate lawyers, too."

"Right. How silly of me." I turned toward Liz and rolled my eyes dramatically.

I wanted her to be in on the joke with me, but she was too nervous to laugh. Men like Dorian made her anxious. She was trying, though. I'll give her credit. She'd told herself that things were going to be different in China, and so she took a deep breath and tried to be different.

She started with a smile. "Lawyers, yeah, ugh. The worst. But *English teachers*? My God, they're the scourges of the city."

"I'm glad you see my point," Dorian chuckled, but looked just slightly off balance.

"I mean, it's like they show up here, completely uninvited, and *force* all these Chinese people to learn *English*. It's disgusting, really. There should be a ban or something."

I laughed. "Supply and demand. She has a point."

"I never said it wasn't a worthy service. It's just not a real job."

"Did you actually just say that teaching isn't a real job?"

He put his hands up, palms facing Liz immediately, the picture of accommodation. "I misspoke. I'm sorry. I meant to say that you're not a real teacher."

Dorian wasn't usually such an asshole. I wondered if sleeping with the new arrivals had gotten too easy for him, if he was trying to give himself a handicap. Or maybe he just wasn't into Liz.

She seemed like his type, though: pretty enough to get a bit of attention from men, not so pretty that she felt she deserved it. Her hair should've been a darker shade of brown, with red highlights maybe. It should've been shorter, too, but she wore it past her shoulders, usually pulled back in a ponytail, like a child. But her eyes were a glassy blue, her neck long and slender, sloping gracefully into narrow shoulders.

I thought about jumping in to defend her from Dorian's barbs, but I didn't. I suppose I wanted them to argue.

"I am one hundred percent not a real teacher. That's very true. I honestly have no idea what I'm doing." She smiled and shrugged, as though her incompetence at her chosen career had nothing to do with her. And then, "Who needs another drink?" Dorian and I both raised our near-empty glasses and Liz set off happily toward the bar.

"I guess she trusts me not to rat her out to the principal."

"Let's have a drink sometime," Dorian answered, ignoring my comment.

"We're having a drink right now." I was still staring after her, allowing the fact of her trust to settle into my lungs, to become a thing I breathed through.

"Not like this. A quiet drink. Or dinner. I haven't seen you in a while. I have some news."

I didn't care about Dorian's news. He'd gotten a new project, or a promotion, or another building he'd worked on was about to open. He'd found a new apartment or was planning to tattoo another ridiculous skyscraper on his arm, this one a still-fictional building that promised to reshape the landscape of global architecture. I'd heard it all and I didn't care.

I cared that Liz had confided in me.

The Chinese might avoid the impulse to relive the past, but I'm moving to Germany, where learning from history is a matter of national survival. There are stories from my nine months with Liz that I can't know, because I wasn't there, or wasn't paying attention. I'm claiming them anyway. I'm telling all the stories I believe to be true.

The first thing that happened was I got very drunk. I wasn't quite dancing on the bar, but I was likely just one Madonna song away. Liz had done the whole frat party thing in college, so what she witnessed as I alternated between margaritas and shots of tequila wasn't new to her. But she didn't know me well enough to question my decision to order another drink, or to lick the salt that accompanied my shot off an Australian woman's neck for the entertainment of the men clustered around us.

Liz spent the time talking to Dorian. I'm not saying my decision to ignore her when what I wanted most was for her to rely on me made any sense. I don't remember it as a decision at all.

"So let's say I didn't want to be a total cliché," she said. "Anything I can do?"

"Move home?" Dorian smirked.

"I'm serious!" Liz protested. "Teaching is a work visa, a way to pay the rent. I admit that. It's not my lifelong dream career. But I still want to get something out of being here. I'm not intending to be a punchline."

"Get a tutor then. Learn the language, something about the culture."

"Is that what you did?"

"I was a Chinese minor in college. I didn't need a tutor."

Liz nodded, made a mental note. She was good at taking advice, and Dorian was good at dispensing it.

She and I hadn't made any kind of pact, and at a certain point, just drunk enough to feel tired, Liz stood by the door, wondering what she should do about me.

"You should just go home. Sasha can take care of herself." More helpful advice from Dorian. "You know the address?"

"I can't go home. I'm still living at the hotel outside the city. I'm just staying with Sasha tonight."

"You're not living with her?"

"No. We just work together. She invited me to happy hour."

Dorian sighed loudly, as he tended to when things weren't as simple as he believed they should be. "Okay, then. We'll have to bring her too."

They both must have turned to watch me, as I spun around in a circle, my arms raised overhead in celebration of some imagined victory.

"Any suggestions as to how?"

Dorian smirked. "We'll trick her." He walked quickly toward the other end of the bar where a small group of expats hovered around me. Liz hurried behind.

He didn't come directly over, and instead rested his arms around the shoulders of two men in orbit around me, leaning in to speak quietly to them. He moved from them to another small group by the bar, and then another. As he made his way around the room, the crowd began to disperse. I remember this night only as the feeling that things were being pulled away from me, that things were happening that I could not control.

"Sasha!" he said finally, as though noticing me for the first time. "Everyone's going to Blue Frog. I'll get your tourist. Let's share a cab." He turned without waiting for me to answer, put his arm around Liz and ushered her toward the door. I remember clearly the drape of Dorian's arm around her shoulder. I remember the pounding of my own heart.

"Liz!" I shouted after them, as though I wanted to stop her from getting on a train and leaving me behind. She and Dorian both turned.

"You should move in with me!"

She was quiet. In my memory, everything was. What I must have sounded like.

"I know you need to find your own place," I continued, trying to slow my breathing. "I know the school isn't helping. I have an extra room." I shrugged then, trying to convey the level of disinterest I had been practicing all week.

"Oh," she finally answered. "I hadn't thought of getting a roommate."

"Great," Dorian cut in before I had a chance to reply. "Can we go home now?"

When the cab that Dorian hailed pulled up in front of my apartment building, he stepped from the car to let Liz and me out and then said goodnight, his hand still clutching the edge of the door. When had he become the chivalrous type? There was a time, not so long ago, when a cab ride home with two women—one of them drunk and the other clueless—would have meant something very different to him. I'd already rebuffed his feeble attempt to ask me out, but the thought of sleeping with Liz must've crossed his mind. I doubt the fact that she was staying with me would've stopped him. In fact, I'm sure a part of him chuckled at the thought of my face, were I to find him the next morning in my apartment.

But he hadn't done it. As the cab ferried him across town and let him out in front of his own building, he must've felt a fleeting moment of pride in himself. But then what kind of asshole feels proud of himself for helping a friend get home? Because we were friends, Dorian and I.

He paused on the dark landing between the sixth and seventh floors of his building, catching his breath. His whole life seemed paused at that moment. He couldn't see where he was going but knew there was nothing to be gained returning the way he'd come.

But then he kept walking, because the landing—which smelled faintly of urine—was not a metaphor.

His apartment was un-airconditioned and stifling. Dorian retrieved a bottle of Tsingtao from the mini-fridge and carried it across the studio, perching himself on the open window ledge where he had a clear view of the alley below. He could've afforded a much nicer place. He was the only non-Chinese I knew who lived in a building without an elevator. But then, he was the only non-Chinese I knew with a sizable savings account.

His meeting with Yang Xue, his real estate agent, was

at nine the next morning. He should have gone straight to bed, should have, in fact, come home immediately after work to review his paperwork and get a good night's sleep. Too late for that now. He was too excited to sleep, anyway; even after the five beers he'd had so far. He wondered how long the process would take, hoped to be moving into a new condo before the holidays.

It had to be Pudong. Shanghai's future was on the East bank of the Huangpu River, and Dorian would be part of it. Everyone in his firm—Dorian included—was helping to shape that future; he wanted to live in it, too. He didn't understand the colleagues who lived in one of the many tiled high-rises dotting the city, or worse the charmless planned neighborhoods on the outskirts, each house a replica of the one next door. Dorian would rather die. He'd be clear with Yang Xue that he needed to live in a building that mattered.

He'd already rehearsed the conversation he'd have with his mother. He'd call to invite her for Christmas, and she'd demure, citing the cost of the flight, the hotel.

"I've saved enough money for your flight," he'd tell her, because it was true. There was down payment money, and flight money, all of it waiting, ready to serve. "And you don't need a hotel. I have a guest room."

"What do you mean, Dorian? Did you move?"

"I bought a condo." He would say it slowly, but without too much excitement, as though talking about a new pair of shoes.

His mother would have enough enthusiasm for both of them. She'd shriek and laugh and ask Dorian to repeat himself, unsure that she'd heard correctly.

"Check your e-mail," he'd tell her. "I just sent you the pictures." Because he'd have cued up the message before dialing her number. Subject line: Check it out.

His mother would scroll through the photos, mostly speechless, occasionally exclaiming.

"Well, I was going to spend Christmas in Arizona with Simon and the kids. But now…I mean, I need to come see your new place. I'm so proud of you!"

Fuck Simon. Fuck the kids, Dorian thought. No, not fuck the kids. His niece and nephew were fantastic. Magnificent. It wasn't their fault that their father was an asshole real estate developer with too much money and terrible taste. But fuck Simon. For sure, fuck Simon. He could bring the kids to Shanghai if he was so desperate for family time over the holidays. Dorian would find him a nice hotel. And Simon would talk endlessly about all the expats getting rich in Shanghai, wondering aloud and often why Dorian wasn't using his connections to open a bar. Simon had no idea what it meant to build something that left a mark. Meanwhile his wife, who was as plastic-looking and generic as the sub-divisions Simon built, would fret over whether the beef and fried onions served to her might in fact be dog, because "don't they eat dog here, Dorian?" and why had the chef been looking at her like that anyway? Eventually Dorian would snap and tell Simon that if he wanted to invest in China so badly, maybe he should spend eight years of his life learning the language and the culture instead of being such an asshole American. His mother would ball her napkin, smooth it out, ball it again, shaking her head without saying anything.

Dorian chugged the last half of his beer in two long gulps. When he finished he let the bottle slide through his fingers past the six stories of windows below him. Everyone who moved to Shanghai complained about the noise; to Dorian it seemed impossibly quiet. The sound of shattering glass filled the night.

6.

I didn't say anything as Liz and I made our way into the building and onto the elevator, her arm around my waist. It took her a couple minutes to open the apartment door—the series of unfamiliar keys and locks confusing—and I slid down the wall and onto the floor while she worked. I wasn't really so drunk anymore, but I pretended, hoping to avoid calling attention to the way I'd ruined everything. She would leave the next morning and never talk to me again. When she finally got the door open she turned to scoop me up off the linoleum.

"Let's get you to bed."

"Don't leave me," I pleaded. "Never leave me." My desperation tasted like vomit. Maybe I wasn't pretending to be drunk.

She helped me into bed, set a trashcan near my head, and went by herself into the guest room. Stripping down, she got under the blanket and lay there awake for as long as she could, watching neon lights dance outside her window. Her old apartment in Brooklyn was over 7,000 miles away, as the jet flies. It should've taken longer to travel so far. Her muscles should've hardened like a marathoner's or atrophied like an astronaut's. Three months earlier she'd been a waitress in Brooklyn, in love and daydreaming about the apartment she and Bryan would finally share. On that night she was an English teacher in Shanghai, slightly drunk and fantasizing about Dorian— the new friend who'd taken care of her that night. If she thought of me at all it was only to wonder how she would extricate herself from my need. At some point before the neon signs blinked off, she made her decision.

The next morning, I lay awake in bed, keeping my eyes closed—just as I did every morning—for one breath, two breaths, three deep breaths. One breath and I registered the headache, faint but throbbing, a hum in the background. It was nothing new. At two breaths I noted that I was still wearing my clothes and immediately pushed the thought out of my mind. Not now. Not yet. Three breaths and I felt my chest rise and fall smoothly, just as it was meant to. I opened my eyes.

Now. Now I could let the world in. I was still in my clothes, but my shoes were off. The drapes were open, and sunlight filtered through the haze which, as always, made it impossible to gauge the time. I heard noises outside my room and remembered Liz, presumably out there pacing, wanting a cab back to her hotel, wondering what the hell was wrong with me.

I consoled myself that the drinking wasn't my fault. I'd been nervous: to suggest that Liz might want to move in, to remain silent. Loneliness sat perched on the edge of my bed, head cast downward like a sullen teenager. I closed my eyes again. One breath. Two breaths. I got up on three, using the exhalation to propel myself through the door. I turned toward the extra bedroom, its door ajar, through which I saw Liz folding a shirt, placing it into the dresser drawer.

"Good morning," I said too loudly, surprising us both.

"Oh, hey. Good morning. How are you?"

She cocked her head and I cringed at the fool I'd made of myself. "I'm good. How are you?" My voice trailed off. I wanted to ask her what she was doing.

"Good." She sounded maniacally upbeat. "I don't have much with me, but I figured I might as well start unpacking. I was thinking I could pick up the rest of my stuff later today?"

"Right. Of course," I answered. I didn't ask her whether she'd changed her mind about a roommate. The answer seemed obvious, and I didn't want to imply that I wasn't happy. The truth was, I was thrilled, but also confused. I'd had my plans, but they'd been ruined by an indeterminate amount of tequila. At the time it was impossible for me to grasp that Liz must have had plans of her own.

"It is really so nice of you to let me live here," she smiled. "I have no idea how I'd find another place, and I think this is really going to work out perfectly."

"Me too." It was the truth. I watched her for another moment. She was still putting away the same shirt; she'd folded it three times, tried it out in two different drawers. I frowned for a moment, still confused, but then caught myself, turned, and headed into the kitchen.

"Do you want some tea?" I called behind me.

"Um… no thanks."

I shrugged, though Liz couldn't see me. Tea for one was fine. Loneliness hadn't come out of my room. I turned the kettle on and leaned against the wall in the kitchen, took one breath, two breaths, three breaths.

7.

Like its inhabitants, Shanghai seemed to hope for something better for itself, the gleaming glass and steel towers of Pudong rising up as though in challenge to the 150-year-old French vision of what China was meant to be on the opposite side of the river. Shanghai had found its own identity since then: a glittering capitalist heart, hardened into a diamond and barely hidden beneath its drab, brown communist cloak. The signs of it were everywhere:

At the 11-story Shanghai No. 1 Department Store, just down the road from People's Square, where young Chinese couples navigated the escalators from the clothing departments up through housewares and electronics, signaling—with each flight ridden and commodity purchased—the strength of their relationships;

On the sidewalks surrounding the luxury apartment buildings on Huaihai Road, where the *ayis* waited at school bus stops for their charges, each of them responsible, of course, for only one little prince or princess, who, at four or five years old had already learned that they should not have to carry their backpacks any farther than two short steps off the bus;

At Xiangyang Market, where so many expats I knew haggled via calculators (or in Chinese, if they'd gotten around to the money lesson with their tutors) for knock-off Gucci bags and Prada sunglasses, and then later, at Carrefour, spent more on French cheese and real olive oil than we paid our maids in a week, feeling equally good about the discounts won at the former, and the exorbitant price of real luxury afforded at the latter.

Constantly under construction, Shanghai was a place to reinvent yourself. This was true for the expats like me and Liz, who shed old selves like so much dead skin sloughed off by our pedicurists, but also, increasingly, for the Chinese themselves, or the young ones anyway, the ones who hung out in the internet cafés and who understood the ways in which small screens, small connections, could increase exponentially the size of their lives.

Liz had taken Dorian's advice for shedding her old self and had found a language tutor, refusing my offer to do it and explaining she wanted a native. Could she tell that I felt sorry for myself as I watched her leave for her first session three weeks after she'd moved in? I don't know how to describe the way the clicking latch of the front door echoed through our apartment after she'd gone. Loneliness exhaled loudly.

Liz had been several times to the Starbucks at Xujiahui; it was one of three that had quickly become part of her regular rotation including the one at Xintiandi and the one at our bus stop, in the ground floor of a luxury hotel, which was, infuriatingly, never open at the posted time of 7:30. Every day of the previous week, she'd stared longingly through the plate glass window into the darkened café, until our bus pulled into the drive and she'd curse the lone employee who clearly had no regard for punctuality and refused to make eye contact through the locked door. I didn't drink coffee, and we didn't own a machine. It never occurred to me to buy one. No—that's not true. It did occur to me, but I assumed if I held out she would break her American habits. She drank tea with me eventually, but she never stopped loving Starbucks.

Liz knew she shouldn't enjoy her visits as much as she did. She wanted everything about her life in Shanghai to be authentic; wanted to fight against the pull of globalism, choosing to ignore—when she thought about it—that it was that very pull that brought her here in the first place. She wanted to think of herself as above it all. She didn't move to China for easy money at a bullshit job, or knock-off purses, despite what her life might look like to an outside observer. She certainly didn't come to drink overpriced American coffee. And yet.

It was an oasis for her, a kind of port she hoped one day not to need. In Starbucks, patrons formed an orderly line in front of the counter, heads craned toward the menu posted in English and Chinese. With a few modifications—the green tea lattes, the lychee Frappuccinos—they offered the same drinks they did back home. The baristas were all either fluent in English, or simply fluent in Starbucks. Tall, grande, soy, skim: they pronounced the words almost without accent. Once clutching her mug—a nice change, the mugs, from the shops back home—she could take a seat in the corner and sit for as long as she wanted. She was not jostled or pressed upon or stared at, as she was on the sidewalks or in the mall. She could take deep breaths and feel herself expanding, settling. I never came with her—one of a handful of mistakes I made in those early days. In addition to not drinking coffee, I was honestly offended by the very idea of Starbucks in Shanghai. I know it made no sense: Element Fresh, on Nanjing Road next to the Ritz-Carlton, where we went for brunch and ordered—from the all-English menu—carrot-apple juice with ginseng, breakfast burritos and French toast, was good, both decadent and somehow necessary. Starbucks was bad. I hung on to the judgment, though, with the vehemence of a 25-year-old.

It didn't bother Liz. After a few weeks in the apartment together, we'd settled into a routine. Starbucks, where she went on Sundays, and sometimes after school, was the only thing that was Liz's alone. She went and ignored my eye rolling, my sighs. At the same time, she hoped that her language exchange would introduce her to new places she'd feel comfortable going to on her own. She would make the request later, after she'd gotten to know Sam. For now she recognized a kind of logic to their meeting at a chain with an atmosphere so uniform and distinct from the rest of the city that it seemed almost to be a country in itself, broken into thousand-square-foot units. It was neutral territory: The United States of Au Lait, The People's Republic of Chai.

Of the Starbucks in her rotation, the one at Xujiahui was her least favorite, but in their initial exchange of text messages, Sam had suggested it and she didn't want to appear disagreeable. The inside of the mall, with its domed roof sitting atop an open atrium, ringed by shops and elegantly arcing staircases going up six stories, reminded Liz of a beehive. The stores were high-end. Having inherited her mother's habit of always checking price tags before size, color, fit, Liz knew she'd never shop at any of them.

While she fought her way through the crowds streaming from the subway entrance in the basement of the mall, and rode the escalators to the third level, wrinkling her nose at the strong smell of ammonia coming from the floors, the windows, the walls, Sam waited at the Starbucks. He tore another tiny shred of paper from the front page of his notebook and rolled it in a ball between his fingers. Returning his hands to his lap beneath the wobbly table, he dropped the ball to the floor, where it landed next to the others. He willed himself to keep his hands on his thighs, succeeded for 30 seconds before returning to the notebook for a fresh shred.

He'd written the date at the top of the page and a title, Language Exchange Session One, as though this were a real class. He didn't know what to write underneath that, though, and so had stopped, but now the bottom of the page was disappearing quickly, shrinking the space he had to write down what she—his instructor? partner? he didn't know what to call her—would say. Maybe he should make some notes about what he intended to teach her. He furrowed his brow, blinking quickly and staring down at his pen. It didn't move, though. I don't think teaching Chinese ever held any interest for him. It was just what he had to offer, his only way in.

On the surface, there was nothing new or interesting in what Sam was doing. All over Shanghai in fact, perhaps at this very moment, expats and Chinese are sitting down at their language exchanges. Some of them use textbooks, or the newspaper; some bring timers, forcing themselves to speak only in Mandarin until the sound of the buzzer indicates that it's time to switch to English. These partners are, quite literally, exchanging language, trading English past tense verbs for the rising and falling tones of Mandarin.

Sam didn't want any of that, though.

He heard the door to the café open and shut, and looked up eagerly, as he had each of the other five times it had opened in the half hour he'd been waiting. Again, it wasn't her. She wasn't really so late, he reminded himself. He'd come early, eager to get out of the apartment and sure the Starbucks would be busy on a Sunday afternoon. He'd been right, but now he felt guilty, holding the table for so long. Three times he'd had to wave away the strangers wanting to occupy the empty seat across from him, hoping, he knew, to drive him out with their loud talk and cigarette smoke. "*Zuòyǐ cǎiqǔ,*" he said brusquely each time, pointing at the melting Mocha Frappuccino he'd ordered for Liz. It's taken.

It should have been more difficult for her to find him—a Chinese man she'd never seen before in a café filled with other Chinese, many of them solitary men. Sam wasn't capable of blending in, though. He wasn't busying himself with his phone, a magazine, or his notebook; instead he stared brazenly at the door, the expectation on his face more suitable for a groom standing at the altar than a man about to have coffee with a stranger. His hair was short but not shaved, and unintentionally fashionable; it lay flat, following the curve of his head in the way of a child's drawing of hair. He combed it carefully each morning and didn't touch it again for the rest of the day, directing his fidgeting fingers to the cuffs of his button-down instead. It was a work shirt, freshly ironed.

Liz waved to him and pointed at the counter, indicating she would buy her coffee first. She wanted more time to think. Do the Chinese go on blind dates, she wondered as she stood in line, because what else would Sam's expression have called to mind? It seemed too personal a question to ask, though. As was typical of Liz, the list of questions she didn't feel comfortable asking was long: How old are you? Where do you live? Have you ever left Shanghai? What do your parents do? What do you do on the weekends? Do you know other Americans? They each spoke to a naïveté she preferred not to reveal.

Before she reached the register she felt a tug on her

elbow. Sam was beside her, close at first until they made eye contact and he took a step back.

"I already bought your drink," he said, turning then to gesture to his table, at which two young women had just sat, pushing Sam's and Liz's drinks to the side. He rushed back to eject them, leaving Liz no choice but to step out of line and follow him.

"How did you know what to order?"

The two women sneered and said something that Liz didn't understand and Sam ignored.

"Mocha Frappuccino is the best. Very sweet."

She thanked him and didn't say she would've preferred a non-fat latte.

"Have you done a language exchange before?" It was an expected opening question, but Sam looked panicked.

"Many times. With many partners." He didn't realize the truth would've been more comforting to Liz than this lie.

"You'll have to be patient with me. This is my first time." She winced at the sexual innuendo she hadn't intended.

"Do you speak Chinese?"

"No. None. I don't know anything." She laughed at herself. It was a relief to admit it. "I don't even know what I'm doing here! I just moved from New York a few weeks ago."

"Why?"

It was another expected question. Before she left, Liz had been asked by the other waiters after she'd given her notice; by her parents—over and over again by her parents—in the weeks that she stayed back in their house in Massachusetts after vacating her room in the apartment she shared in Brooklyn while she waited for her departure date; and by Bryan who found the decision more confusing than anyone.

She'd tried out a few answers so far. I really like dumplings, she'd told her co-workers. They laughed, and none of them pressed for a serious answer; they didn't really know her, didn't care where she moved.

She'd told Bryan that she needed a drastic change, which was closer to the truth, but still didn't really answer the question. Los Angeles would have been equally drastic, but she hadn't considered that, or any other U.S. city, for even a moment.

It's a really good job opportunity, she'd told her parents. But that didn't explain why she'd gone looking for it in the first place.

"Where did you get this idea?" her mother had asked her one night, as though it were a disease she'd picked up somewhere.

Liz had only shrugged. Having moved back into her old room, if only temporarily, she felt obligated to communicate like she were 16, though she knew it wasn't helping her cause.

But then, she didn't know what to say to her mother that didn't sound like an indictment. She wanted bigness for her life, but didn't that make her mother's life sound small? She wanted freedom, but didn't that make her mother sound like a captor? So she shrugged and sat silently through the dinners her mother cooked, and her mother didn't push because it wasn't her way. Some nights at the table she looked proud, other times devastated; Liz ignored her.

What would her mother have said if Liz had returned home in a week, two weeks, having lost the great job opportunity? She cringed, and saw Sam squint, as though concerned about her. She remembered where she was and reminded herself it wasn't time to dwell on what she couldn't control. The deadline laid out in the green envelopes to hand in her lesson plans had passed. She'd tried to write them several times but didn't know where to begin. How could she explain that to Principal Wu? Instead she waited, wondering what would happen next.

8.

In the months since she left, I haven't given much thought to these early days living with Liz. They were never the problem, or at least that's what I'd always thought. I didn't talk to her about the green envelopes, the deadlines she was missing, because I felt it important that she come to me first. She sat with those anxieties much longer than I thought she would. It should've been a clue.

But back to Sam's question, the why of her move that it took me weeks and weeks to finally ask. She must have tried to give him a real answer, eager as she was to make a good impression. "I wanted to do something no one would expect," she said, simply, answering truthfully for the first time.

Sam's eyes widened. "I'd like to do that, too." Just like that he was hooked on her, in the same way I was when I'd first read her application and created in Liz the solution to Loneliness.

There was an awkward pause, as Liz wondered perhaps if she had revealed too much. Or not enough. But it was all for today. For the next 20 minutes, she fired off ideas for things they could talk about during their next session, as though it hadn't occurred to her that they might actually begin today. Just by talking to each other.

"I could probably bring in some newspaper articles that we could read and discuss. Or I could find some grammar lessons, I guess, though that's not really my strong suit."

"My grammar is not a problem," Sam answered, pronouncing his words a bit more slowly.

"Yes, of course," she said. "So…what do you want us to do?"

He remained silent for a time. The truth was difficult, and if the exchange went well, he hoped he'd never actually have to say it.

"I want to know what it's like to be American," he responded finally.

"Okay. I can talk about that." Her tone suggested that they'd settled something larger than they had. "I need you to start at the beginning with me. The alphabet, or characters, I mean. Or whatever is the beginning. I know nothing. I don't even know what I don't know."

"Tones," Sam told her. "We'll start with tones."

"Right. Four of them, right? Four ways to say every word?"

"No," Sam shook his head. "Just the opposite. Only one way to say each word."

She frowned. "But I thought…"

"There are four tones, plus neutral, but for each word in Chinese, the tone never changes. You don't have four different ways to say a word. Just one way for each word."

"But you might have one word, spelled the same, but with four different tones? Four different ways to say it, and that changes the meaning?"

Sam shook his head more quickly and frowned. "There really isn't spelling in Chinese."

"Um...okay."

He leaned over his paper, frowning for a moment, before drawing a quick horizontal line, slightly thicker on one end: 一. This character, *yī*, it takes the first tone, high. No other tone goes with this character. It is fixed."

"What does it mean?"

Sam continued drawing, without looking up: 以. "This character, *yǐ*, takes the third tone, falling rising."

"But you just said the same word. *Yī* and *yǐ*."

"Different words. Different characters. Different tones. Different meanings."

"Okay, but if you were going to write them, like in English?"

"In English? *Yī* means one. *Yǐ* means to use."

"Oh, no, I mean if you wanted to write them in Chinese, in the Roman alphabet, though, no characters."

"Pinyin."

"Yes! Pinyin. They are spelled the same, right?"

"Yes." Sam wrote Y-I down on the paper. Twice. With different accent marks.

"Okay. So they're the same word, just with different sounds."

"Okay," Sam sighed. "Yes."

Liz smiled.

Sam put away his paper. "More tones next time then?"

"Yes! Tones and conversation."

They made plans to meet at the same time next week. Sam rose abruptly. "*Zàijiàn*, Liz. Goodbye."

"Bye, Sam."

He must have wondered, as he hurried out of the coffee shop, whether he should have made her repeat the Chinese after him. He hated teaching Chinese. This was, of course, his first attempt, and it had only lasted 10 minutes or so, but already he knew he hated it. It wasn't entirely his fault, though. Liz was a terrible student.

Sam walked, without thinking, to the park across the

street from the shopping mall. He should have brought her there. Teaching would have been different without a table between them. There were no *lǎowài* in the park today, but he'd seen them there before. The expats, in fact, often outnumbered the Shanghainese, who thought of the park as somewhere to walk through, on their way to someplace better. Expats sat, lounging on the grass or tossing a Frisbee back and forth until the men in brown uniforms came with their whistles, hurrying them off the lawns. They were never with Chinese, but that didn't mean it wasn't allowed. Sam and Liz could have sat beside each other on a bench, and when she asked why everyone around them was staring, Sam would explain that they were all *jídù*, jealous, of him. Second tone, rising; fourth tone, falling.

It was not the way to learn Chinese, but it was all that Sam could think to do. Here is a word. I will give it to you. Hold on. Here is another word. Take them from me and you will owe me something in return.

Yī: one.

Lǎowài: foreigner.

Yǐ: to use.

Jídù: jealous.

9.

One blossom. Two blossoms. Everywhere there are lonely people drinking tea. Shanghai is no exception. Everywhere there are lonely people holding their breath and listening for the sounds of their own heartbeats, wondering how an organ that is nearly smothered can be so impossibly loud. One blossom. Two. The lonely people brew their tea and then sit and watch the jasmine flowers floating slowly up from the bottom of the cup, blinking their eyes, listening for their smothered hearts.

I wanted my blossoms to mean something. Maybe they did. Maybe by focusing my attention on them, I gave them power. I'm watching, I whispered against the lip of the cup. I'm waiting to learn. Willingness was enough, I'd decided. Or anyway it was all I had to give.

Noticing things gave them power. Saying them aloud made them true. It became my philosophy during those early weeks with Liz. I started waking up earlier than necessary to give myself time for tea and mantras.

"I've always been an early riser," I told Liz. "I just love

the quiet time in the morning. It's really important to me."

Saying things aloud made them true.

Liz respected the quiet, treated my morning tea almost as a religious ceremony. After three weeks, though, I grew impatient. I hadn't learned anything; nothing had changed, except I was more tired, and I suspected that Liz thought me strange.

Four blossoms. They were tiny buds, dried and rolled tight, and then unfurling in the near-boiling water. Growing into themselves.

"Do you want some tea?" It was the first time I'd offered. I was tired of waiting for her to ask. I was tired of waiting for so many things from Liz, but tea was the place I started.

She'd emerged from the bathroom, her hair still damp from the shower and pulled back into a ponytail. I remember thinking that she'd look much better if she blow-dried.

"Do we have time?"

I looked at the clock. Seven-fifteen. The bus picked us up at 7:30, no exceptions, no waiting for anyone. "Probably not." I sighed. "You should get up earlier. We could have tea together."

"Yeah," she answered slowly. "It might be nice not to be so rushed in the morning."

"Or, whatever." I knew she had no interest in having tea with me. I felt stupid for having suggested it. "You should get up whenever you want."

"No. It sounds nice. Thanks." She slipped past me into the kitchen to grab a bottle of yogurt, then carried it with her back into her bedroom.

Things were strange, but I didn't know how to fix them. On the surface it was all just as I'd expected: we walked to the bus together in the morning, sat in the same seats— Liz by the window, me the aisle—ate lunch together in the school cafeteria. On Wednesday afternoons, when the weekly staff meeting kept us late, we sat in the back of the auditorium, whispering complaints about the wasted time, though we never had anything else to do. Once home we would go shopping, or watch DVDs; some afternoons, Liz would sit in Starbucks. I chose the dinner spots—mainly the more expensive Western restaurants frequented by all the other expats. We went to the happy hours, too, and out dancing. We were roommates and friends, just as I'd hoped.

Loneliness had vacated the apartment, but she'd been replaced by a jasmine flower called Anxiety. I watched it gently unfurling, beautiful and meaningless. Noticing things gives them power.

I didn't know yet why Liz had moved to Shanghai. I wasn't like the rest of them, expecting some kind of logical or concrete reason. But I wanted her to recognize that about me. I was waiting for her to admit things to me, over dinner and a bottle of bad red wine: *I don't know what I'm doing here, or what I'm doing with my life.* I'd planned the dinners, and ordered the wine, but Liz had never said anything like this.

I looked at her often in those early weeks, trying to match up the person I knew with the person I thought she was when I'd read her job application. Nothing made sense and I didn't feel any better. We left for school that morning just as we always did. I left my solitary mug in the sink.

10.

Shanghai practically sizzles in the rain. Large puddles form at intersections and run in rivulets along the curbs; the pedestrians plod through them, undeterred by the rainbow slicks of gasoline floating on their surface, the congealing soot along their edges. It's the same soot they blow from their noses or hack into their handkerchiefs as they wait for their busses, stepping back at just the right moment to avoid the spray from the taxis that career past with occupants still patting dry their hair, wiping their necks with their own grey-stained rags.

The fat raindrops pummeled the sidewalk as our school bus crept along the congested roadway, inching toward the highway. Liz sighed and closed her eyes. She'd resolved to talk to the principal. The day before I'd left another green envelope in her mailbox, another deadline for handing in more lesson plans, along with another quote: *Deal with issues from a place of inner peace.* She took the message personally.

The question of course was how to deal with the issue.

She couldn't admit to the principal that she had no lesson plans at all. Most days she decided on the bus in the morning, or even as she walked toward the classrooms, what she would do with her speech students. Today, for example, she was going to have them list words that rhymed with "cake" to write on the board. Then they'd draw pictures. She'd have to lie to the principal, tell him that she had plans but that they weren't written down in a form that she'd be able to hand in. It would at least buy her some time.

I heard her sigh, but I didn't ask her what was wrong. Though I'd gotten what I wanted—Liz had moved in and on the surface we were friends—I still felt uncertain about how she saw me. I couldn't understand why she hadn't asked for help with the lessons yet, or at least complained about the enigmatic notes. What else could I conclude except that she didn't trust me after all?

I wanted to tell her my stories, but I didn't know how.

"The first time I ever tried to masturbate…" I wanted to say with the hint of a smirk on my face. But I couldn't.

It was August, hot and muggy, and I'd retreated to the cool air and new carpet smell of the basement rec room. I was 14, bored and entitled. I took off my shorts and lay on the new sofa in my underwear and a tank top, feeling bold, but also nervous, my ears attuned to any noises upstairs. Why I wasn't locked in my bedroom or the bathroom I can't really say, except perhaps that I was looking for danger.

My fingers had only grazed my inner thigh when I saw the spider out of the corner of my eye. For a moment I thought it was a cartoon. It was too large, anyway, to be a real spider: hovering on thin legs at least two inches off the ground, it might as well have been wearing ballet shoes. Its abdomen was the size of a ping pong ball. My stomach turned, turns still, whenever I think of that tiptoeing monstrosity, so out of place in a suburban house outside New York City. Leaving my shorts where they'd pooled beside the couch, I got a spray can of Raid out of the garage, crept as close to the thing as I was able, and emptied the bottle. As the white foam slowly coated its body, it lurched and tipped on its legs, but continued moving toward me. I was sure I heard it gasp. I panicked then, found an aluminum mixing bowl to set down on top of it, trapping it and leaving it to die slowly, like everything else in Westchester County.

I ran halfway up the stairs before putting my shorts back on.

Four days later, when I finally had the courage to return to the basement, the bowl and the spider were gone.

But it will never leave me. I see now the gaping holes I was expecting Liz to fill: my loneliness and depression, my anxiety. But I didn't know what else to do with them.

Our bus pulled into the driveway of the school.

"I hope it stops raining."

"I don't mind it, actually," Liz answered.

"Are you kidding? It's like acid falling from the sky. Don't let it touch you." We filed off the bus and hurried inside, where Liz followed me into the main office.

"Did you need something?" I asked, sounding hopeful.

"Oh, I, uh…I need to talk to the principal."

"You're not quitting, are you?" I spoke out of fear but wanted to swallow the syllables as soon as they'd left my mouth. It was the last idea I wanted Liz to get.

She was quiet for too long, then laughed. "No, nothing like that."

I stood there for a moment then, waiting for her to tell me what the meeting was about, but Liz stayed silent, unable to admit her failures.

"I'll see if he's free," I said finally. A moment later I waved her back.

"I am glad you are here," the principal said when she stepped into his office. "I need to talk to you."

"You do?" It must have occurred to Liz that she would

be fired. She sat heavily, already resigned to her fate.

"You have found a new address?"

"A new address…" her voice trailed off. "Oh, yes, I, uh, gave it to the, uh, housing person right after I moved." She couldn't remember Serena's name. "I know I was a couple days late, but I had some trouble finding—"

"Late. Yes. So I imagine you are here about the fee."

"The fee?"

"You stayed beyond your scheduled departure date. I can give you credit for one of the days. The rest will be taken out of your pay next week."

"How much is it?" It seemed like the thing to ask, though the numbers were virtually meaningless to her. She made more than she needed for basic living expenses; if the fee was coming out of next week's pay, then it was less than a week's pay, and therefore not of any concern.

The principal shuffled some papers around on his desk, as though he perhaps had the number written down somewhere already. "You will be informed of the amount," he answered finally. "It is for the hotel room."

"Okay."

"Excellent." He stood abruptly and gestured toward the door. "Thank you for coming to see me about this."

He ushered Liz out of the office before she had a chance to tell him that it wasn't at all what she'd come to see him about.

Later that afternoon, a green envelope appeared in her mailbox in the staffroom. She carried it back to her desk to open, checking first to see if anyone was watching.

The cat who chases two mice catches neither.

She sighed and opened the card without attempting to interpret the quote. On the inside she read: ¥600. That was all. It was just a bill for the extra days she spent in the hotel room. The principal had told me to inform Liz what she'd be charged; he didn't specify how.

Surprising herself, Liz tore the note in half then,

momentarily stunned by her power to do so. Ripping it into four more pieces, she smiled and dropped the confetti in her trash bin. She looked at the rest of the envelopes still stacked in her desk, and for a moment thought about just tearing them up too. But what would that solve? There was no fee she could pay for being bad at her job. She knew she'd have to do something about the lesson plans, soon. For now, she had a class to teach, and so she headed out of the staffroom, listing as she walked the words that rhymed with cake.

The next morning my alarm went off at six, as always. First, I thought about hitting the snooze button—once or twice or three times—until I'd be forced to fly out of bed, shower quickly if at all, run out the door to make the bus. Then I thought, for the first time since Liz had arrived, about turning it off entirely, staying in bed for the rest of the day, turning off my phone. The fact that I didn't do this was a good sign, of course, but also deeply troubling to me. Sometimes I wished I could have made more of a commitment to my depressive instincts, but I seemed unable to play the role correctly.

I forced myself out of bed and into the kitchen, thinking not of the demands of my job, but of Liz. That was the whole point of a roommate, after all. She was, without knowing it, a life raft that I had stepped into; I didn't yet have a comfortable place to sit, but that was no reason to step off the boat, allow myself to sink.

Fixated on this Liz-as-raft image, I floundered around, wishing for a pillow and maybe a book to read, and so was startled to enter the kitchen to find Liz-as-real-person-in-bathrobe standing there, pondering the tin of Jasmine tea.

"You just dump it into the cup?" she asked in lieu of a greeting.

It took me a moment to realize she was talking about tea, that she had, in fact, gotten up early for this, just as she'd said she would. "I like to watch them bloom," I answered finally.

If she thought the response strange, Liz didn't show it. She simply pushed the tin toward me, and leaned against the wall opposite the stove, waiting for me to take over.

"I'll bring it to you," I told her. It was the least I could do.

The kitchen was a narrow alcove, separated from the open living room and dining area. Liz backed out, leaving me with the tea. She went to sit at the table in the other room and I moved slowly through the tea-making process, wanting time to consider the implications of this new development. On one hand, we were just roommates, having tea in the morning before work. On the other... But no, there was no other hand. We were just roommates, and it was just tea: a normal beverage, a typical morning activity. Yet I felt a fluttering in my gut. I thought again about the spider.

I poured the water. In my head I listed all the things I would never say aloud to Liz. The jasmine flowers bloomed and I named them: Agitation, Timidity, Dread. I thought about the hopes I'd had before Liz arrived—that my depression would disappear if I had someone else relying on me. To a certain extent I'd been right, but I was left with the realization that I could lose everything at any moment. It was a feeling I recognized.

You must be in love with her.

I stared down at my cup, as though the rogue thought had emanated straight from the blossoms. Three weeks and they had finally spoken.

I carried the hot cups of tea into the other room, trying also to carry the equally hot and fragile thought, unsure where or when I'd be able to put it down.

11.

Love didn't run around at night, searching the faces reflected in plate glass for someone she used to know. Love didn't get her feet dusty, couldn't tolerate the creep of grime up her shins, the slick of puddles on her soles. When Love stood quite still, as she so often did, she could feel the pull of mountains and rivers and half-constructed skyscrapers and eight-lane highways and movie theaters and the quiet parks with their untouched grass circling around her bowed head.

Was I scared of Love? Of course. In my experience she was overly forward and easily frightened, the cause of both self-doubt and delusions of grandeur. But maybe this time things would turn out differently. Isn't that what people always believe?

I believed it, anyway, so I sat with Love in our living room. Welcome to my heart and would you like some tea? Liz paid our new roommate no mind. For two weeks Liz and I shared the jasmine tea—Love didn't drink, but she watched, very intently, waiting for something to happen.

I wondered how to get Liz to notice her. Loneliness was nowhere to be found.

Love came to work with us every morning. I worried about the chill in the air and wondered if I should loan Love a coat, naked as she was, her skin nearly translucent, almost bluing, the color of skim milk spilled onto a grey Formica countertop. We arrived at school and while Liz went to teach her classes, Love curled up under my desk. I covered her with a blanket and fretted over the noise in the office, played soothing music from my tiny computer speakers, told Principal Wu the melodies had a proven effect on worker morale.

I knew that left unrequited, Love could never be happy. But there were limits to what I could do to satisfy her. Love spoke softly, and so I tried to quiet the world around us. I stopped making plans to go out. No more drinks at O'Malley's or Zapatas, Blue Frog, or M on the Bund when we were feeling fancy. No more dancing at Park 97 or Guandii. No more house parties with costume requirements. Fall edged closer to winter and I promised Love we would hibernate.

Forsaking all you can eat hibachi and late-night dumplings, I decided to fatten us at home. I went to the grocery store every day after school, dragging Liz along with me, offering half-sentence explanations about saving money as I perused the produce aisle. To affect the fearlessness I believed Love required, I bought long beans and bitter melon, bamboo shoots and taro root.

All things are difficult before they are easy. I wrote the Chinese proverb down because I believed it. I tucked it away in my wooden box and taught myself to cook. Most nights we ate late.

"Why don't we go out?" Liz suggested more than once, but I usually refused. Love was too fragile to entrust to a crowd of expats, and though Western women were rarely the focus of anyone's attention, I still felt as though I had to protect Liz if I had any hope of keeping her. She didn't go without me. I believed that meant something. There were the afternoons when she walked to her sessions with Sam, and others when she brought a book to Starbucks to unwind by herself. But she always came home for dinner.

Until one night she didn't. I set the table for two, but the plate across from me remained empty. Love sat beside me, tapping a long fingernail against the oak table.

"I think I've finally mastered the texture of the Chinese eggplant," I said.

Love rolled her eyes.

"And the chicken tonight is particularly moist."

Love pursed her lips and stamped her feet. She sighed loudly.

"Okay!" I shouted. And then more softly, "Okay. I know." I started to cry because I knew I had failed Love. She patted my shoulder and cleared away the dishes anyway.

While I sat in front of our chicken dinner that night, Liz stared out the window of her cab, trying to put our lonely apartment out of her mind. Traffic lurched past the open green lawn she didn't realize was People's Square, which she didn't know was the center of the city. She only saw the grass, and the trees edging the paved walkways, curiously lit up from their bases with green and blue lights. She was reminded suddenly of the trip to Disney World she'd taken with her parents when she was in fourth grade, of the Polynesian Village where they'd stayed.

And so she found herself passing slowly by the circular Shanghai Museum, devoted to the ancient art and culture of the country, and thinking only of a child's token, a fake coin used to buy an imaginary treasure. There were more clouds that night, thick and heavy, low in the sky and refracting the neon from the city just below, seeming to glow from within. Liz wished for a rumbling thunder, a change in the wind, but there was nothing. She thought of me again, as her car rolled past the park and picked up speed. Me, cooking. Me, searching for something Liz could perhaps help me find. It was a generous thought, and it was gone in an instant.

She turned her mind then to Dorian, wondering what he thought of her. For instance, was this a date? She'd searched my phone one morning earlier in the week while I was in the shower, copied down Dorian's number, sent him a text: Want to grab some dinner? This is Liz. Texting was perfect for Liz—how lucky for her to have stumbled into a culture where it was the only means of communication. But it meant she had no idea whether Dorian was surprised to hear from her or not, whether he paused and stared at the phone, struggling to place her name, whether he smiled and answered quickly, having imagined the invitation in the weeks leading up to it. He texted back: Sure. And then: Hong Chang Xing, North Gaungxi Rd, famous hotpot. Liz didn't know what that meant. She only knew she and I had never been.

The idea of trying to get to the restaurant on her own terrified her, but she wasn't about to ask me to write down the address for her. She had the pinyin and remembered the lessons Sam had given her in pronunciation. So far in their sessions Liz had been staving off any actual grammar or language instruction by filling their time with practical questions: "How do I take the subway? How do I pronounce these streets?" She was working toward independence rather than fluency.

She watched nervously out the window as the cab continued through the evening traffic, wondering how long it would be before she could glance out at the Shanghai sidewalk without feeling overwhelmed. Just glance and turn away, to look at her phone or think about what she would order to drink that night. The key, she thought, was perhaps more understanding: Tell me why they post the newspapers in glass cases along the sidewalk, and I will stop having to notice them. All of the noticing was exhausting. Liz wanted to get to the point where she stopped having to see every detail, where she could just live her life.

This is what her language lessons should focus on. After only a few sessions, she'd already decided that she would never actually learn to speak Chinese. She hadn't told Sam, but she assumed that he knew. But she didn't want to stop going.

Sam, just make this normal for me, she wanted to say. Just tell me why. Why do the Chinese squat on the edges of the sidewalks? What are they waiting for, and why doesn't the posture hurt their knees? Why do they walk backward through the parks? Why do cabdrivers have one long fingernail? Why do teenagers stop her on the street to ask—in English—for directions to nearby and obvious places, and then giggle when she answers? Why are there decibel meters—huge signs—posted along the streets if no one seems to do anything about noise levels? Why is there always the crackle of firecrackers in the air?

Listing all of the things she didn't know about her new home exhausted her. She probably wouldn't end up asking Sam any of these questions, though, or me or Dorian, either. There are books and books and books of words that Liz and I never spoke to each other; our insecurities differed only in their coloring.

Had she asked me I would have told her that there were no answers, that it's impossible to explain away an entire culture. This wasn't an archeology project. This was just life. So no, it wasn't about understanding, but rather just acceptance. Just get used to it, Liz. Just live here, and soon you will stop seeing so much.

The cab stopped in front of a building that was

possibly a restaurant, perhaps even the right restaurant: the Chinese characters glowing neon above the door made it impossible to tell. But Liz paid the fare and got out, hoping for the best. Thirty minutes later, she was pleasantly buzzed on warm sake and not-quite-cold beer and plunging thinly shaved beef and mushrooms into the vat of boiling water between her and Dorian, having forgotten all about me.

"So what's with the tattoo?"

Dorian pushed up his sleeve, smiled like someone just asked him to tell his favorite joke.

"You like it?"

Liz cocked her head to one side, a whisper of brown strands skimming her cheek.

"Was a giant penis on your forearm too obvious?" She could say things like that and no one ever got mad.

"Yes, yes, skyscrapers are phallic symbols. Very original."

"Don't worry. I have a Georgia O'Keefe replica around my belly button, so we're even."

Dorian laughed. And because she made him laugh, he told her the truth:

Taipei 101 wasn't the most amazing building in the world, and it wasn't the only skyscraper Dorian knew would end up tattooed on his body. At one point, he told Liz, one of those tattoos, those buildings, would be Dorian's design. He didn't want his own building, though, to be his first tattoo, or his last. So he had to choose some others. Dorian was a planner.

Liz also knew when not to make a joke. She took a well-timed bite of sizzling Chinese cabbage, dipped in the peanut soy mixture Dorian had concocted in one of the small white bowls between them. Imagine creating an entire meal by dripping messily from one pot of sauce to another, flavoring your next bite with the remnants of this one, and you understand hot pot.

"That's either endearing, or the most narcissistic thing I've ever heard."

"Couldn't it be both?"

They got along well, mostly because Liz was content to let Dorian talk.

"It's interesting, I think, to choose to live in a place where you'll always be an outsider."

"What do you mean?"

"I'll always be a *lǎowài,* no matter how long I live here." *Lǎo* can mean always, he explained to her, *wài* foreign. "A *lǎowài* is always a foreigner. It's actually kind of a derogatory term, but I like it." Dorian loved Shanghai for its capacity to accept foreign influence—in its architecture especially—without being conquered by it. Shanghai took what it wanted and made it its own.

"Ask your tutor about *lǎowài* versus Shanghailanders," he instructed her, referring to the term for Westerners living in the city before the communists took power. "Get a native perspective on the role of foreigners and how it's changed." Dorian liked to give homework assignments.

"How do you know I got a tutor?"

"You're a smart girl." Dorian winked. He was always winking.

Liz imagined not for the first time what it would be like to sleep with him. It wasn't Dorian specifically, though. Just someone different from what she'd known. She came to China for something different.

"His name is Sam. So far he's been great."

"Wait, he's a guy?"

"Yeah. So?"

Around them conversation swelled. At each of the white Formica table tops with their centerpieces of boiling broth, diners sat hunchbacked, their knees too close to their tables and their chests, the chairs the wrong height for the tables. Or they were all leaning forward to dip their shaved beef, their tofu and mushrooms, watercress and snow peas. The chatter sounded angry to Liz, the way Mandarin can if you don't understand it.

"How's his English?"

"Surprisingly good, actually. I don't feel like I'm teaching him much."

"Has he taken you to the mall yet?"

"You mean like shopping lessons?"

"No, I mean has he tried to buy you a dress? Or a new cell phone?"

"Why would he do that?" Liz asked with food in her mouth. She did that sometimes, but only when she was comfortable with someone, when she wasn't paying attention.

"Because he wants to date you, and that's how Shanghainese guys date."

"He doesn't want to date me! Why would you say that?"

"He speaks perfectly good English and still wants to do a language exchange. What else could he want?"

Liz shrugged. "He told me he wanted to learn more about America."

Dorian laughed, loudly and for a long time. Then he took a sip of beer. He didn't say anything else.

Liz crossed her arms, pretending to pout. "That doesn't mean he wants to date me!"

Dorian raised his eyebrows.

Liz laughed. "Fine. Maybe he wants to date me. But so what? He's still a good language partner." She pretended to be annoyed by the suggestion, but really was flattered. Didn't it mean Dorian thought she was datable? Could it mean he wanted to date her?

She spent the rest of dinner and her cab ride home wondering about Dorian and Sam, what they might want from her and when she'd find out, what she would do when she did.

12.

I finished cleaning up, because there's nothing more pathetic than a woman sitting amongst the detritus of a ruined dinner. I left the wine out, though, because drinking seemed my only option. Sipping wine and staring at the front door, I rehearsed my opening lines:

"I was worried about you."

Or, "I thought you'd be home for dinner."

Or, "How was your night?"

Or, "Well, well, well..."

Or, "Howdy."

As it turned out, I had a mouthful of wine when the door finally opened; I swallowed quickly, then hiccupped, and coughed.

Liz gave me a funny look. "Hi," she said slowly, looking as though she expected me to pull a weapon from under the table.

I tried for nonthreatening, wishing I had a book beside me, or at least my phone: anything to disguise the blatant desperation that shrouded me.

"Wine?"

She looked relieved. It was, I guessed, a normal thing for me to have said. I poured a glass as she sat down beside me.

"Long day?" she asked.

"Weird one," I answered, and then, after a sip for courage, "Weird few weeks, actually."

"I was wondering. Have you cooked everything in China yet?" She laughed, and I realized she was drunk. This was probably a good thing, but I couldn't help but feel jealous.

"What did you do tonight?"

"I had dinner with Dorian," she answered after a long pause, and I heard in her voice an apology.

"Oh." It was the only hint of disappointment I allowed myself.

There was silence while we both looked into our wine glasses.

"What did you do?" she looked around the room, as though there might be evidence of something.

"Just hung out for a while. Read a bit. Cooked some dinner." Cooked you dinner, I wanted to say, but stopped myself.

"Are you boycotting restaurants now?"

I laughed nervously. It was time to talk about it. "No. I'm sorry..." My voice trailed off while I had another sip of wine. I wished I'd had more to drink while I'd been waiting. "I had this crazy idea." Even as I started the sentence, I wasn't sure which crazy idea I was going to admit to: that Liz maybe was also in love with me; that if she wasn't already in love with me, she would fall in love after tasting my efforts in the kitchen; that love was just a matter of proving certain skills—cooking just a kind of elaborate mating dance.

"I wanted to make things homier around here, you know, so you wouldn't get homesick and leave." It was plausible enough.

She laughed. For what seemed like hours. "Don't you think you should have asked me what I missed from home before you started trying to recreate it?"

It might have sounded chastising, or mocking, but she was smiling and sipping wine so I chose to think she felt touched.

"Okay, so what do you miss?"

"I don't know..."

Say snuggling, I willed. *Say secrets in the dark.*

Liz's long brown hair fell over her face as she stared down at the table, and I longed to grasp it between my fingers, pull it toward me, and tickle my own chin with it. Her fingers tapped against the stem of her wine glass, and I longed to lick them, imagining they would taste like honey.

"There isn't much I miss," Liz answered. She didn't look up at me. If she had she would have known. "I don't really feel homesick, at least not yet. Just really disoriented, I guess."

I nodded. You're dizzy and I can catch you. Maybe we should go lie down. Instead I refilled her glass.

"You'll get used to it."

"Right. Of course."

We sat in silence. I hated roommate small talk.

"Why did you move here?"

She laughed. Her laugh. God. Like glass shattered in ecstasy. "I was wondering when you were going to ask me that."

"It's such a boring question. I usually try to avoid it. But it's weird, I guess, that I have no idea."

"Yeah. It's weird that I have no idea either."

I shook my head. "I don't buy that. You're not the type to move across the world on a whim."

"Right. So what type am I?"

"You're more thoughtful than that," I answered slowly. I wanted my words to stick, to have a hand in shaping her. "You have plans."

She looked at me then like she was finally seeing me for the first time. "It was more of anti-plan, I think. Everything in my life had been so predictable, you know? Graduate from high school and go to a mediocre college near the really good college where my high school boyfriend was going. Date for four years and then follow him to New York. Let him pay for dinners because he's making tons of money working in finance while all I can find is a wait-ressing job at a shitty diner because what the hell do you do with a degree in English anyway, if you don't want to teach, and I really didn't want to teach."

"But you're teaching now."

"Right. But teaching isn't really my job here."

"Living in China is your job."

"Exactly. I wasn't *doing* anything in Brooklyn. I'd left my town, but my life wasn't really any different than it would've been if I'd stayed."

It was the most I'd ever heard her say. I got up and opened another bottle of wine.

"What happened with Mr. Finance Boyfriend?"

Liz shrugged. "Bryan and I started dating when we were 15. It didn't seem possible that we'd end up together."

"That must have been really hard. Did he end it, or did you?" I wanted to hear her heartbreak, or her defiance.

She gave me neither. "It was mutual. I wanted some kind of new experience and he was committed to his job, so this just made sense. It wasn't some kind of big emotional thing. It was just a logical decision."

Love didn't solve equations and while she did occa-sionally deal in absolutes she felt much more comfortable ensconced in cotton, her outer edges blurred, her center held fast but difficult to find. Bryan and Liz didn't know this, but I did.

"So, you and Bryan broke up, and the next obvious step was move to China?"

She laughed. "Yeah, that's the part where the logic gets

fuzzy. I knew I wanted to get out of New York, but I didn't know where to go. Going home would have been defeat. Anywhere else in the States, I'd need a reason, a plan. It seemed like moving abroad was a plan in itself. I took the first job offer I got."

"Cheers to that," I clinked my glass against hers. "I'm glad you're here." This time we did make eye contact, and I made the most of it, shooting sparks.

"Thanks. Me too."

I love you, too, is what I heard. I wanted to lunge across the table, but somehow managed to restrain myself. "We should have more wine," I said instead. "And sit on the couch." I felt like a teenaged boy waiting to yawn and stretch my arm across my date's shoulder. Ridiculous, but somehow it was working. Liz sat down first, and I sat close beside her, leaving almost an entire cushion of the couch empty. She didn't fidget, though. She didn't look uncomfortable.

We kept talking and I looked for reasons to touch her.

"Your hair is really beautiful." I actually said that, and then waited for Liz to cringe and slink off the couch, back to her own bed, away from me and my creepy compliments. But she didn't move. Or, she didn't move away from me; instead she turned and leaned back, flinging her hair across my lap.

"Oh, do you like it?" she laughed, shaking it.

"Yes, very much," I whispered, but she didn't hear. She was drunk and laughing, had collapsed completely onto my lap. I was afraid to move, afraid to ruin it. I did run my fingers through her hair, though; I couldn't resist. Liz closed her eyes and purred like a cat. I closed my own eyes, too, focusing on the feel of those strands.

It may seem that Love gets lost easily, wandering off

after the aroma of pork dumplings, pan-fried and served steaming, or running frightened from the crash and pop of fireworks meant to scatter only old ghosts. Most of the time, though, Love stays put; if she seems lost it is only because she can be hard to recognize.

"Have you ever been in love?" Liz asked.

I could've told her about Alice, whose gloss-coated lips turned me into a child with the sticky remnants of elicit candy around my mouth. After Alice there was Heather, who tasted of mushrooms sometimes, other times grapefruit; who rubbed peppermint lotion into my feet, up my calves; whose metallic green car reflected the sunlight off its trunk as she drove away.

"No," I answered, because the truth was too complicated to explain.

"I have," she replied, and I shrugged.

"Have you ever had sex with a stranger?"

I snorted. "I mean, not a complete and total stranger, 'I don't even know your name' kind of thing. But definitely 'I just met you tonight and we've talked for an hour, and I'll never see you again.'"

"I haven't." She wasn't pausing for stories. "Have you ever had sex in public?"

I blushed, but Liz's eyes were still closed, so it was okay. "Are we playing this game now?"

"Yes."

"Fair enough. Semi-public, I guess. Have you?"

"Yes. Your turn."

I knew exactly what I wanted to ask. Two more questions and I'd do it.

"Have you ever had sex in a car?" I said.

"Yes. You?"

"Yes."

"Have you ever had sex on a plane?"

"No."

"Me neither. I almost did once."

Don't tell the story, I thought. Don't say his name.

"Your turn," she pressed, and I exhaled loudly.

"Have you ever kissed a woman?"

"No," she answered, and I could tell from the pause at the top of her breath that it was a different kind of no. "Have you?"

"No, but I've always wanted to." This was a lie I shouldn't have told.

"Me too!" Liz squealed and sat up. She was so drunk I wondered for a moment if I should stop the game. But I believed because I wasn't a man, I had nothing to force on her.

"So...should we?"

"I suppose we have to," I answered.

"Okay, wait." Liz adjusted her posture, pulled her hair away from her face, licked her lips. "Okay, I'm ready."

I leaned forward; Liz met me halfway. We pressed our lips together, softly: top lip on top lip, bottom on bottom. At first we didn't move. She was like a child, playing at something she didn't understand. And then suddenly she understood. Our lips parted and I pushed my tongue through until I felt the gleam of Liz's teeth.

We separated a moment later, the kiss that satisfied the constraints of our game complete. We looked at each other, for just a second, and then leaned in again. Have you ever kissed a woman a second time? Have you ever run your tongue along her jawline before pressing your mouth to the quick pulse in her neck?

I paid attention for signs of hesitation—a nervous laugh or a gasp that sounded more like terror than plea-sure, a flinch or a pulling away—but noticed none. My fingers lifted her shirt slightly and touched her waist, tracing delicate patterns of curling ivy around her belly button. In response she ran her hand up the back of my neck, nestling long fingers around the roots of my hair and pulling, not so hard that it hurt, but it surprised me nonetheless. I was expecting more timidity from her. I raised my eyebrows in a question and she smiled, pleased with herself. She kissed me again, then crossed her arms around her waist, touching my fingers still resting on her stomach as she did. In one fluid motion she raised her arms over her head, uncrossing them as she did, and removed her shirt.

"You should take this off," she whispered, tugging at the bottom of my shirt, surprising me again. It was the first either of us had spoken since the game had ended. Or maybe this was still part of the game.

I felt the sudden urge to retreat to my bedroom, where the curtains blocked out the neon twilight shining through the windows. I wanted to bury us under my thick comforter—never mind the sweat—so we could feel but not see our bare legs pressing against each other, our soft bellies, our breasts. I was afraid to pause, to give her any time to question what we were doing, but I was more afraid of staying where we were. Though our living room was entirely private, our front door locked, I felt too exposed.

I took her hand and stood up. It could be a test—a chance for her to giggle and hiccup and tell me she was getting sleepy. But she hooked her finger in my belt loop. She followed me to bed.

Love remained curled at the end of the couch, slicked with sweat and shivering.

The next morning when I woke up she was gone.

SUCH A THING IS POSSIBLE

爱

I wonder now about the wisdom of all this remembering. I snap the clasp of Liz's necklace behind my neck, the weight of pearl on my collarbones both familiar and uncomfortable. Her parents had given it to her when she graduated from high school. It seemed an old-fashioned gift, and she hadn't known what to say when she'd opened it. "You can wear it tomorrow," her mother had chirped, "and then on your wedding day." Liz somehow managed not to laugh. She left it in its box on the kitchen table that evening. Her mother knocked on her bedroom door later that night, the necklace in her hand.

"I know it probably seems like a silly gift," she said before she even sat down.

Liz shook her head. "No. It's beautiful."

"My parents gave me a pearl necklace for my high school graduation. And I really did think of it as the thing to wear whenever I did anything really important." She undid the clasp, holding the end pearl in her fingertips and letting the strand dangle. "I started to think of it as keeping track of my life."

Liz wasn't sure what to say, but her mother seemed content to continue talking. "So, for you, here," she pointed to the first pearl, "is the day you were born. Here," grasping the second pearl, "is your first day of school. Do you remember I made you that little grey pinafore dress? With the scalloped edge?"

Liz nodded. Her first day of school was lost to her, but she remembered the pictures: the grey dress looked something like a school uniform, but it was hers alone. She suddenly remembered her backpack—purple—and the three multicolored folders she'd tucked inside, all of them empty. She smiled, and her mother continued counting off pearls: her first period, the day she started high school, her first job. She surprised Liz with the specificity of her memories. "And here is your graduation day, tomorrow," her mother finished. "But you see there are so many pearls left." She took Liz's hand in hers and let the necklace fall into her palm, patted her thigh, and left.

Liz laughed when she told me the story, and I couldn't tell at the time if she was laughing at her mother or herself. She brought the necklace to China, after all. Wore it on her first day of school.

And then she gave it to me.

Love is a storyteller. Creating new realities, giving substance to memories previously mere wisps of smoke, she talks and talks and talks. Some of what I said was even true.

"Once, when I was five years old…" I said.

"Once, when I was 17…"

"Many times in high school…"

Liz listened to everything. I got drunk on her attention, let myself believe I was safe.

I told her about the afternoon when I was seven and

my father had taken me to Serendipity, in the city. I'd gotten dressed up and had wanted to order a fruit tart because it looked delicate and grown up inside the glass case. My father pushed me to choose the hot fudge sundae, perhaps wanting something he knew would take me a long time to finish. He'd started up with his "ums" and "ahs" when I was just a few bites in, and as he kept talking I began shoveling larger and larger bites into my mouth, barely stopping to taste the ice cream or the chocolate sauce, feeling only the sticky film developing on my hand and the end of my spoon and around my mouth. I'd left the cherry in the bowl. When he finished talking, finally, and I finished eating, we both sat staring at it, so red it was almost obscene. He'd asked me then if I was going to eat it, as though it had been any other day and any other dessert, and I'd leaned over and thrown up beside the table. The vomit looked like some lunatic's idea of happiness, just like my parents' marriage.

He hadn't told me about the secretary, but then he married his cliché and I figured it out.

"You must have stories," I said after the moment of silence that followed. It wasn't what I wanted to say.

"We have ham every Christmas," Liz offered. "My mom always cut the end off before cooking it, and I could never figure out why. One year I finally asked and she didn't know. She said it was how her mother had always done it. So I asked my grandmother at dinner, and it turns out she always cut it off because the only pan she had was too small to fit the whole ham. My mother was horrified." We both laughed. "That's what passes for scandal in my family—years and years of wasted ham."

I wasn't sure how to interpret this.

If not for the all-you-can-drink plum wine special the restaurant was running, I might've had the sense to remain quiet.

"My father got me into college," I said. "His money. His *connections*. I was one of those girls. I squandered the opportunity, just like I squandered everything else he ever gave me, nearly flunked out. My shrink intervened on my behalf, thank God, and late assignments were accepted! Credits were awarded! The debutante was allowed to graduate."

"Why are you talking like that?"

I should've known better. "Ha Ha, You're a Failure" was not a dinnertime story. It was meant for the stage. My portrayal of the Dean of Arts and Sciences really couldn't be beat. The role of my father was played by an angry voice on the phone: "What exactly am I paying for here, Sasha? What exactly are you doing?"

"It's difficult to discern, father, what precisely I am doing, exactly, as I have been consuming mass quantities of Goldschläger, which you should be aware, has been very difficult to procure but is necessary as I feel the ratio of cinnamon to gold flakes perfectly mirrors my chemical composition at this time. And though the good Doctor Smith—whom you are so generously paying for and so thoughtfully calling every day and pumping for information about me despite my alleged doctor-patient privilege (which I suppose is waived when you're not the one writing the checks)—prefers I don't drink the stuff. But you see, father, I feel it is essential."

I couldn't say all this with a plate of *gŭlăo ròu* between us. The restaurant smelled of oranges and chilies, and the air felt slightly greasy; the sizzle and pop of splattered oil in the kitchen was audible over the clacking of dishes and the low hum of conversation around us.

I shrugged in response to Liz's question and stared down at our pork, the crispy edges of the meat, the pale orange sauce glistening provocatively. "Defense mechanism I guess."

She didn't ask what I was defending against. Maybe things would have been different if she had.

We went to that Chinese restaurant down the street

from our apartment at least once a week. So maybe I could've staged my performance there. I might've just called our waitress in advance, the one who looked too young to have a job and who giggled whenever Liz ordered in English, as she did often, forgetting that I needed to speak for her. We will need the table in the corner, I might have said. The one next to the strange little stage where you keep the potted plant. Please seat the gentleman who is always grunting at his noodles in the back. I didn't call, though, and didn't deliver my stirring final monologue.

"You tell me a story," I sighed.

Liz picked up a piece of pork between her chopsticks, circled it around the bottom of her plate, tracing a path through the viscous sauce, parting the green peppers. "Once upon a time, I moved to China and met a girl named Sasha."

"I think I've heard this one before."

"I can't help it. All my stories started when I moved here."

I pretended to look annoyed. "Just try one."

"I can tell you more about Bryan, I guess."

"Ugh. Bryan. I'm so sick of Bryan. Can't we do some kind of voodoo ceremony, light him on fire and move on?"

"You're the one who asked for a story!"

"How about college other than Bryan. What else did you do?"

"Just normal college stuff. I went to class, sometimes skipped class, went to parties."

"Did you have a best friend?"

"Not really. Freshman year I hung out with my roommate and the other girls on my floor, but then they all pledged. I was off campus so much, hanging out at Amherst with him. I didn't make many close friends."

We were silent for a moment. "Sorry," Liz continued. "I know it all sounds terrible. It wasn't, though. Just average."

I smiled and nodded, as though this was all I wanted.

I was trying to be encouraging.

Meanwhile, Love stared down at the cold pork and its congealing sauce, feeling slightly sickened, and sad for Liz and me: Two women who shyly bared our inadequacies, real or imagined, watching each other for the slightest flinch.

We held hands as we walked the three blocks back to our apartment building. It was a side street, a quiet one with not too many neon signs flashing. Liz looked up at the sky, and then stopped, began to laugh.

"What?" I asked.

She laughed again, then shook her head. "I was expecting to see stars," she said. How stupid of her.

In the 10 months since Liz left Shanghai, I haven't allowed myself to look for her online. But now that I've opened the box, have clasped the necklace around my own neck, all promises to myself have been broken. My laptop is packed in my carry-on; in a few clicks I am online, searching the internet for her constructed personas.

Liz Fabrio reveals nothing, but when I try Elizabeth, there she is.

She looks thinner, her cheekbones cutting angles that in all the nights I spent watching her sleeping face, I never saw. She's bronzed and powdered, red-lipped and shimmer-eyed. Her dark brown eyes have been lined by a professional hand, and her hair sits in wavy piles atop her head, its caramel highlights reflecting the light. She is smiling for posterity, and with the knowledge that in this picture her flaws will be airbrushed away, as only a woman on her wedding day does.

Dusk on a Sunday makes Love want to weep. She compensates for the suffocating quiet with microwave popcorn. She has loud orgasms. Dusk gives way to night and Love feels better. Or Love compensates by making a family, filling her life with people who drown out the hush.

I'd heard all those noises in Heather—the salty crunch of popcorn and the cumming and the raucous future I believed we'd have. To my father's ears, though, it must have sounded like a girl being murdered.

He'd burst into the room in a panic. Through the door she and I had forgotten to lock.

I heard all the noises again in Liz. Really I did. Such a thing is possible twice.

1.

Sam hovered near the wall of the Starbucks. Each week that Liz didn't cancel he was surprised. It seemed so improbable that he'd found a language partner who also lacked an interest in exchanging language. Liz asked her questions about the subway and the produce in the grocery store she couldn't identify, but she was unmotivated to do the kind of intensive study required to speak Chinese. Sam assumed she wanted something else. He'd never thought of himself as a lucky person before, but maybe that was changing.

On the morning that Liz crept out of bed without waking me, Sam scanned the tables for a sign that someone might be leaving: a hand going for a coat, or pushing away an empty mug, a sigh and an uncrossing of legs. Several patrons, still clinging to their tables and the last sips of cold latte, had forecast the wrong signals and were now stuck with other customers standing uncomfortably close to their chairs, tapping their fingernails against their own mugs, talking too loudly. He and Liz didn't stand a chance.

After launching in Taiwan just a few years earlier, and then Beijing, Starbucks spread to Shanghai and other parts of the mainland. The company learned that most Chinese preferred to come in the afternoon, sipping the sweeter drinks they favored over coffee as they lingered around the tables or couches. Sitting still conveys status in a city where time to be squandered is a luxury; there's nothing to be gained from bustling out with a paper cup in your hand that would anyway be spilled in the first rush to board the subway or the groaning bus. The Shanghainese who go to Starbucks have the time to stay, smoke, talk loudly, and gesture wildly with sunglasses resting atop their heads and shopping bags at their feet.

"Wow, busy."

Sam looked over, surprised. "I didn't see you come in."

"How could you? It's a mob scene in here. Should we go somewhere else?"

"Maybe we walk?" He was nervous to choose another place. There was a tea house nearby that would be empty, but they'd be on display, the waitress hovering, indiscreetly listening to their conversation if she understood English, speculating loudly in Chinese if she didn't. Is that his girlfriend? she'd ask. How much is he paying her? And then laugh. Liz would ask what she said and he would lie. Ignore the *xiǎojie*, he'd tell her. The waitress. But the word also means prostitute.

No, they couldn't go to a tea house. Walking they were exposed to the same kind of scrutiny, but at least if they kept moving he wouldn't have to hear it.

"What are the coffee shops in America like?" Sam guided them west out of the mall, away from the tangled intersection of Hongqiao, Huashan, and Hengshan Roads, which would be filled with people heading to the shopping mall, the subway station, the movie theater complex around the corner.

"Not so different," she answered slowly.

Sam pictured cavernous spaces, the tables separated by wide aisles, where customers sat reading newspapers, ignoring everyone else. This was all of America as he imagined it: quiet, with enough space: to drink coffee with anyone, or walk down the street holding hands with whomever you wanted. "They must be different." He didn't know where they were going; he just wanted not to have to walk with his elbows up, deflecting the crowds. Turning off the main thoroughfare, they walked past tall apartment buildings and more than one real estate agent's office.

"Well, they don't come around with free samples." She paused. "And there aren't so many Chinese people in them."

He said nothing, waiting for her description to conform to his hope for what was possible. She was incapable of telling that kind of story, though.

"Not that there is anything wrong with Chinese people," she rushed.

Finally, he laughed. "There are just so many of us!"

Liz laughed too. "Well, yes, I guess, but that's not what I meant. It's just strange to live somewhere where the vast majority of people are the same race. In New York everyone looks different. No one stands out."

"You grew up in New York?"

"I moved after college. I grew up in a small town in Massachusetts. Do you know Massachusetts? Boston? I lived sort of near Boston."

"I know about Harvard," he answered. "And the Red Sox."

She laughed. "That's pretty much it."

"Everyone looks different there, too?"

"No," she paused, "they're all white."

"You're used to fitting in." It wasn't a question.

Liz shrugged. "Sometimes fitting in means disappearing."

What Sam wouldn't give. It had nothing to do with

race, he wanted to explain. But he didn't know how. He would've argued with Dorian's point that Shanghainese were insiders while the *lǎowài* were always outside. Or at least he would've pointed out that being born in Shanghai—being able to blend in on the sidewalk—did not mean he was free. He pictured himself in a coffee shop with Liz, either in New York where he wouldn't stand out, or in her hometown where he would, but for reasons he could live with.

It took me a long time to realize Sam and I were looking for Liz to save us from the lives we didn't want to live.

They continued walking in silence: awkward for a language exchange. The street they were on was quiet too, mainly residential. Above their heads, laundry hung on ropes strung between the trees and power lines.

They had to step off the sidewalk to avoid a group of older men blocking their path with rickety chairs and an overturned milk crate set between them like a coffee table.

"Why do they do that?"

"What?" Sam had navigated around the group without seeing them.

"Just sit out on the sidewalk like that."

He shrugged. "Their apartments are very small." Inside, they'd have no view of the street. They'd have missed, for example, the young Chinese man walking beside a *lǎowài*, a woman. He and Liz would be fodder for the rest of the day. "They like to see what's going on." He barely contained the disgust in his voice. Neither the groups of men in their public living rooms nor the waitresses in the tea lounges were really Sam's problem though. To disappear from their view—as he did when he was out with his friends, as he would if he were walking with a Chinese woman—was relatively easy.

Escaping from his family was the real magic trick. Communal property was a pair of his pants draped over his own chair in the corner of his own small bedroom; his mother went through his pockets. The aunties heard about his promotion before his workday had ended. And they all knew a perfect Chinese girl for him. All those perfect girls he didn't want.

They crossed the street. The day was crisp but sunny, and the park they walked into was filled with people: clusters of teenagers, a handful of young couples, and the elderly, alone or in pairs.

"Do you have a boyfriend?" Sam asked, keeping his eyes on the sidewalk.

Liz wasn't sure what to say. She thought about my hands leaving prints in her skin, as though she were made of clay. She thought of her own lips, bitten and bruised.

"I had a boyfriend, before I moved here. But we broke up."

She paused, waiting for Sam to ask what happened.

But he wasn't interested in Liz's past. "And now?"

She shook her head. "I have...well, it sounds crazy to say. Or crazy for me anyway," she laughed nervously. "I guess you could say I have a girlfriend."

She kept her eyes on Sam, waiting for a dropped jaw or a smirk, a searching glance that he'd try to hide. But he kept his face forward, either because he wasn't surprised or he was too polite to show it.

"Oh," was all he said, and then after a moment of silence, "I'm happy for you."

"Thank you," she said. "I'm happy too." She didn't stop to wonder if that was true. But she wanted it to be.

She didn't really have a girlfriend—not technically anyway. Not yet. But Liz was impatient and unconcerned with technicalities. Just like Sam, she'd been looking for an escape from her old life; in my bed she thought she found it.

2.

I'd woken that morning with the taste of Liz still on my tongue but found only a long brown hair on the pillowcase where her head was supposed to be.

My hopes rose like a balloon: that she was in the kitchen making tea, wearing my t-shirt and nothing else, still smelling like our sex and waiting to kiss me good morning.

My t-shirt was on floor, though, and the kitchen was empty. My hopes were inhaled helium—making me sound ridiculous. I crawled back into bed and pulled the covers up over my head. Smelling Liz on my pillow I started to cry.

My tears were dry by the time I heard the front door open and close. I didn't get out of bed. She would tell me, I was sure, that last night had been a mistake. She would tell me she was moving.

I wasn't prepared for her to come into my room. She didn't knock, and I don't know if she knew I was home.

"Sasha?" she said as she sat down on the edge of the

bed, beside the unmoving lump that was me. I didn't answer. I didn't really think I could hide from her, but I also wasn't ready to face her.

My silence made no difference. She pulled the covers back slowly. My cheeks were tear stained, eyes puffy, but I tried to project a sense of calm. "Are you going to leave?"

Prior to coming to Shanghai, Liz wasn't a person who pursued what she wanted. Bryan had been in her sophomore English class. They'd sat next to each other, and a few weeks into the term he'd asked her to study for a test with him. Then invited her to a school dance. Then kissed her. Their relationship followed a typical path. Bryan picked her up and Liz got in the car. Bryan made requests and Liz acquiesced. Bryan got into a top college and Liz went to the state school nearby. Bryan pledged a frat and Liz bought formal dresses to wear to his parties. Bryan got a job in New York and Liz found an apartment in Brooklyn. As long as Bryan kept asking, Liz kept saying yes. You didn't say no to a boy like Bryan.

But I wasn't a boy like Bryan.

"What? No," she said. "No. No, I'm not leaving. No." With me, no was always easier for her than yes. She continued to repeat it as she reached out to touch my cheek, as she leaned down to kiss me. I pulled her into bed, unbuttoning her jeans as I did, tugging them down awkwardly and then rolling her onto her back. I knelt over her, self-conscious for a moment as I fumbled with the denim around her ankles, and then her pants were off. Using the neck of her shirt I hoisted her to sitting again, then lifted it up over her head. It's back was damp with sweat and I wondered if she'd hurried home.

"Tell me what you like."

I love you, is what I meant.

"I don't know," she answered, and then: "I like you."

I believed her. Everything I did made her moan or gasp or whisper "fuck" in my ear. She pulled down on my shoulders as we kissed, carved shapes in the mattress with the moon-shaped heels of her feet as my tongue traced new stories on her inner thighs, as my fingers curved inside her like a comma. I felt her pulse inside my mouth. After she came, her breath still ragged and her hands covering her face, I said, "I'm going to make you do that again." And I did.

Afterward, we lay in bed beside each other, dozing, still not speaking. An hour passed, or maybe two—enough time for the sweat to dry, for new sleep to form in the corners of our eyes.

Liz took a deep breath. "I think I'm going to be fired."

I laughed, laughed and laughed, my face still buried under covers. Finally I peeked out and saw the look on her face. "Wait, you're serious?"

"Can I still live here if I don't have a job?"

"You're not going to be fired. Why would you be fired?"

She sighed and got out of bed, walked naked and without any shyness out of the room and returned with her stack of green envelopes. She set them down in front of me and climbed back into bed, only then looking embarrassed as she buried herself under the covers.

I didn't need to read the notes, but I pretended, allowing my eyes to glance over the carefully chosen quotes and series of deadlines to hand in the lesson plans—all of which had passed.

And then I shredded them: a grand gesture of their meaninglessness, of my power. I was surprised by how long Liz had kept them a secret. Long before I fell in love with her, before I learned her contours with my tongue, I expected the notes to bring us closer.

It was too late to tell her that I wrote them. Maybe

after we'd been together for years I'd tell her of my first clumsy attempts to become part of her life. For now I only promised that I'd take care of it.

The next day—the first day that Liz and I woke up in the same bed—I waited until the principal went to lunch and crossed his empty office, to the tall metal cabinets in the back where the archived lesson plans were filed. Ms. Felisha's plans only went back a year, but there were plenty of them (she'd been fired, but not for insufficient planning).

I stared at the thick folders, one for each month, wondering how many to take. I wasn't sure I'd have time to photocopy the entire year's worth of plans before the principal returned from his lunch. There was always the possibility, too, that Liz would use these plans as a jumping off point and begin writing her own lessons. I settled for three months, knowing I could always come back if I needed to.

Folders in hand, I rushed to the photocopier, and only as I stood there, listening to the whir and whoosh of pages through its gears did I realize the risk I was taking. It occurred to me, as I imagined the principal bursting back into the office, demanding an explanation, that I might have simply helped Liz to write some original plans. But then the humming of the photocopier ceased, and I stood in the empty office holding the warm stack of new copies in my hand, smiling and thinking how much easier this was. It made no sense that the school demanded that speech teachers reinvent the class each year; Liz deserved the plans.

Later that day I set the stack of paper down proudly beside her tray of shredded pork and rice. Our table was in the corner, equally removed from the screeching students and the other teachers huddled together, their backs to us—the two Americans. It used to bother me, but not anymore.

Liz stared at the papers for a moment. I waited, not wanting to have to say aloud what I'd done. Finally, she seemed to realize what she was looking at. "Are there—oh my God, are these what I think they are?"

I only nodded.

"Where did you...How did you...? Never mind. I don't even want to know. Are these for me?"

"Of course they are."

"So I can hand these in? I'm not going to be fired?" Liz looked as though she might burst into tears.

"You're not going to get fired," I laughed, pleased that I could offer her such relief. The cafeteria echoed with the clanging plates and bowls, the shouting of students.

Liz picked up the stack of papers, flipping through them, her mouth hanging slightly open. "I'll hand them in right after lunch. Who do I give them to?"

"Well, wait—you can hand them in, but you're going to have to re-type them, and you know, change them around a little bit."

"Oh. Really?" She looked disappointed.

"Liz, they have another teacher's name at the bottom of them!" I pointed at the bottom of the first page, and then the second.

"Oh, okay. Right. So...what do I need to do exactly?" She asked like she'd been given extra homework assignment.

"You know—make them your own. Change the dates, and the formatting. Rearrange the order, maybe. Or change a few of the activities." I leaned forward then and lowered my voice. "I took these out of last year's files for you. I don't think anyone will remember them, but I can't be sure. You have to at least make them look different."

Liz nodded her head, tucking the papers into her bag at her feet. "Thank you so much." She sounded significantly less enthusiastic than she had moments ago.

"You're welcome. So you'll get to them this afternoon?

I know it's a little tedious, but we want to make sure you get them in as soon as possible. You're way behind on the due dates." I didn't really think Liz would be fired, or at least not without me knowing about it first. But there was a point at which I knew it would be too late for me to save her. If she continued to miss deadlines to turn in her plans, Madeline would eventually notice and say something to Principal Wu, who would in turn say something to me. I looked at Liz, thinking of the nights we'd had together, and became increasingly nervous. What would I do if she was fired, if she had to go home?

"Um…yeah, I should have some time this afternoon, I think. I have a free period later. I could go to the computer lab."

There was nothing in her tone to reassure me. "You know what?" I held out my hand to her. "Why don't you give them back to me. I have tons of free time this afternoon. I'll take care of it."

"Really?" Her face brightened once again. "Thank you so much. I just can't believe you'd do all this for me. I really appreciate it." She handed the papers back to me, seeming relieved to be rid of them.

I was even more relieved to have them back in my hands, their weight a comfort to me. I never should have brought them to Liz. "I'll hand them in for you. I'll just give them to Madeline. Just ignore any more notes asking for them. I'll take care of it."

Liz smiled and thanked me again, tapping her foot against mine underneath the table, sending sparks up my leg.

At the time I felt in control.

3.

Love doesn't sleep, but instead at night blinks more slowly, head tipped back, looking for fresh air. She can spend 12 hours like this, picking up the scent of the only flower for miles. November in Shanghai could still feel like Spring. Love could be forgiven, squinting as she did as the sun cracked the horizon, for mistaking the intent of the breezes, for expecting new life to burst from the ground at any moment. I was tricked in those days as well, remembering how morning used to feel: like I was lying under a thick concrete slab, only my head, fingertips, and toes sticking out the sides, just enough room in my chest for gasping, shallow breaths, and not enough strength to move. That November, though, with Liz lying beside me, there was lightness and space. It was Love, after all, that had cured me. Liz-Love. It was magical.

In her sleep, Liz's lips parted slightly, not in a disgusting, drooling kind of way, but in *A Midsummer Night's Dream*, "I've just taken a sip of this nectar and am waiting for you to kiss me," kind of way. As she woke, she sighed and wiggled her butt back and forth, as though chasing after something, or preparing herself for something new. I always wondered what she dreamt about. Liz could never remember or was horrible in the retelling: "You were there," she would say. "Everything was blue. And sort of fuzzy. We were somewhere different." *What did it feel like*, I wanted to know. *What was it like when I touched you?*

At that point, I hadn't had a single dream about Liz, which told me that our relationship was the first real thing I'd ever experienced. That I was always in Liz's dreams, however, didn't concern me. I felt like a conquering army: triumphant.

On school mornings we woke like roommates who happened to share a bed. We learned quickly that a joint shower would cause us to miss the bus, so we agreed to take turns, and as we brushed our teeth, I stopped grasping at her waist from behind, pressing just hard enough on the sensitive space below her hip bones to make her gasp and catch herself on the sink as her knees buckled slightly. I stopped hinting in the morning at what my hands could do.

"You look pretty today," I would say instead.

"Thanks." That was it. Liz didn't say "you, too," because I'd explained to her how I hated that—the reciprocal compliment—for the sense of duty it dragged along with it.

Work days were easier—for the rules, the map of decorum we had to follow—but also agonizing. The school bus especially. I never told Liz about the very first blowjob I gave, in the back row of a school bus, 15 years old and on a dare, while the boys in the seat in front of me pretended not to look but did and I pretended not to know that they looked but did. Here we were again on a school bus every day and I just wanted Liz to run her fingers through my hair some mornings, make reassuring sshhhhing sounds.

But she didn't know any of that and I thought it was for the best.

Liz hadn't gotten any better at her job. I repeatedly offered her copies of the lesson plans I reformatted and adjusted each week, but she always refused, happy to continue talking with her students about their favorite foods, favorite places, favorite books, ideas she always came up with on the bus on the way to school, or sometimes in the hallway before class. I never wished that she were a better, more passionate teacher; she was passionate about me, and that was enough. The job, though, was important to our lives together, a necessary piece of our puzzle. My careful work on the lesson plans was one way to keep it safe, but I knew it also needed to be protected against Liz's whims, understanding as I did her hatred for it.

A year ago, January in New York, she was trudging to work through the slushy streets of Brooklyn, trying not to wonder what Bryan would be doing later that evening, without her, once he got off work, trying not to wonder when he might propose, trying not to think about how much of her life revolved around waiting: waiting tables, waiting to get engaged, waiting for something to happen to her. A year ago, she couldn't look directly at any of it, for fear that she would crumble under the weight of waiting.

And then. January in Shanghai: it was cold but had not snowed. Likely it wouldn't, I told her. In January only the wind howled, racing through skyscraper-edged tunnels. In January the tourists haggled for knock-off pashminas that they wrapped once, twice, three times around their necks, feeling exotic though the wool was cheap and scratched at their chins. In January the space heaters got turned way up, or they didn't get turned up quite enough, and every-where people were either warm and dry and chapped, or shivering in their bones as they sat in restaurants and bars. Liz and I burrowed, like everyone else, but I was the only one who didn't want to come out.

In January the new year lay ahead—12 months of promise and prosperity—its luck guarded by the loud popping of fireworks, the jingle of cymbals on the dancing feet of dragons and lions. I insisted we clean the apartment: the wisps of dust swirling behind the couch, the grime on the windowpanes, all the corners and crevices that would have been easier just to ignore. Liz seemed glad for it.

We nestled into the clean apartment, hibernating within the warmth we created around each other, coming up for air and food and work. I thought it was what we both wanted.

But I know she didn't understand my dark moods: they came on suddenly, like a migraine, and required the same gloom, the same silence. Are you in pain? she might have wanted to ask, but she never did. She likely told herself she was respecting my space, but really she didn't want to know the answer. She stayed quiet, bundled up.

Part of her had imagined a different kind of expat life, though, the China Famous kind. Expats were famous for opening popular bars and clubs—for stocking American beer and knowing how to cook a hamburger, for playing current music, for offering deals. The ones who did it with style were famous just for going to the bars. They were famous for karaoke. For their house parties. Two women like us could've been China Famous.

I had different fantasies, though.

"Can't you just think of it as a treasure we are guarding?" I asked her one night.

"Treasure is meant to be squandered."

"I don't want this to be squandered," I whispered.

"That was a joke."

We didn't talk about it often—only a handful of times,

maybe—but when we did, there was always a punchline. Really we were having a two-month long fight, but my wit allowed us to laugh instead of cry.

During all this time Love sulked. She resented being treated like the comforter at the foot of the bed. Love didn't shout though, didn't rage. She didn't even stamp her feet. Instead she sat in the chair in the corner of the living room—the white one with tassels hanging off the piping that edged its overstuffed cushion. There was a fake plant behind the chair, and a lamp that didn't always work. Love sat there, tapping her fingers.

I appeased her with sex, trying to get to the point when she was no longer performing. Liz liked to have her back scratched, would sigh and rock her hips when I ran the flat of my fingernail from the base of her spine to the bend of her neck. She liked the crescent of her shoulder kissed. When she was drunk she'd dig her fingernails into my hands. She'd run around the bed and laugh. When she came she closed her eyes.

Outside the apartment we seemed like best friends, walking close to each other on the way to the bus stop, moving at the same pace, sometimes holding hands—if there were only Chinese around—because in Shanghai, girls held hands sometimes and no one thought anything of it. We sat with heads bowed on the bus, laughing, speaking our own language. Once at work we had jobs to do, but those barely interfered with our time together. Liz had all but abandoned her desk in the staffroom amongst the other first grade teachers who still glared at her and barely spoke. She spent her free periods sitting at a small table just behind my desk—no one in the office seemed to care. If I was busy she went to the computer lab.

There were still days when I could not get out of bed. It surprised me, assuming as I had that Love would cure me. But when I heard Liz on the phone, explaining to the principal how both she and I had come down with a terrible stomach flu, I realized that Love was with me after all. Liz left me alone to sleep, and then brought in lunch and a set of DVDs for us to watch together. In this way, winter wore on.

4.

Though I never accepted his invitations and sometimes didn't even answer them, Dorian kept asking me out. Who knows when or why he'd become so thoroughly convinced that I was the one he wanted. Maybe only because it seemed he couldn't have me. Clichés are often true. He didn't know me well enough to fantasize about inviting me to live in his new condo with him, but still he pictured me there. At a barstool in his kitchen. In his steam shower. In his bed. In his mind they were all his, not ours. Dorian didn't know how to share, which might have mattered if there weren't so many other reasons we never would have worked.

He focused only on the fact that we were both still living in Shanghai after three years. We made it, he would tell me. This is what we get. As though we were contestants on some kind of reality game show: Who Wants to Live in China? We do! We do! Our living room would become a kind of expat salon. We'd end up in the next edition of *Let's Go Shanghai*: When traveling through the city, one must stop and visit Sasha and Dorian for tips on the best dumpling houses and a coupon for 50 percent off a martini at Blue Frog.

It's hard to say if Dorian even wanted this, or if he just couldn't imagine any other alternatives. A Chinese wife? An endless adolescence—years and years and years of happy hour and screwing the English teachers? He was past all that, he knew, but where did that put him, if not in a new condo with me?

He imagined, as he picked up his pace covering the last few blocks between his office and apartment, going back in time to the moment when his choices ceased to be limitless. Would he be able to spot it, if he knew what to look for? It was called adulthood, he guessed: that moment when the sum total of all the decisions he'd already made began to shape and define the available options. What had he been doing during that moment? Drinking a beer? Or sitting at his desk? Not realizing that there was no longer any room to move sideways. It was obvious to him that Liz hadn't yet crossed this threshold, and he thought about befriending her, so he could watch for it, could jump out at just the right moment and tell her: *Haha! There it was. That was the last decision. Everything else now is consequences. Enjoy!* And he would bow with a flourish, as though he'd just performed some kind of magic trick.

Thoughts like this didn't always depress him. On the day he'd first met with his real estate agent, he'd felt as though the pieces of his life were finally falling into place, building a path. But on walks home from work he realized a path is really no different than a wall. Same bricks, different placement. The real estate agent hadn't taken him around to look at any properties, and in fact looked at him like he was crazy when he'd asked.

The first appointment was meant to test his seriousness: Yang Xue spent 45 minutes explaining to him everything that could go wrong during the process:

Chinese apartments were very small; he might not like any of them; the one he liked could be sold to someone else; the newest buildings would take too long to be built; his offer might be rejected because he was a foreigner; the government might confiscate his apartment; he could lose a lot of money. The list went on and on until he wondered how Yang Xue managed to make a living; weren't real estate agents, after all, in the business of selling hope? When she was finished she asked him cautiously whether he'd like to set up another meeting.

He'd been excited prior to the second one. He'd heard her warnings, had proven that he would not be deterred. Again they'd never left Yang's office.

"You brought a copy of your bank statement?" she'd asked when he sat down.

Dorian nodded and reached into his bag, pushing the paper toward her proudly. She glanced at it quickly and sighed.

"This does not have an official stamp."

"What do you mean? I got it from the bank. They printed it for me there."

"Yes, yes, of course." Yang bit her lip and looked down. She remained silent longer than Dorian could take.

"There is a problem? Something else I should have done?"

"Yes, a problem." She sounded relieved that he mentioned it first. "There is an office. The Official Documents office. They need to provide a stamp of authenticity."

"But how will the office know the statement is authentic?"

Yang didn't answer, so Dorian asked instead how to get there.

It was not open on the weekends, and so he'd taken off work to stand in line. There were three, actually: one to receive a number, a second to pay for the stamp, and then another to wait for his number to be called (this last being a physical line, even though each person in it was holding a number dictating their turn).

Now, finally, he was back in Yang's office, officially stamped bank statement in hand. She was surprised that he demanded Pudong. It wasn't yet a neighborhood many people wanted to live, but Dorian knew—better than even Yang did—how fast that would change. On site visits with his firm to the sprawling new district east of the Huangpu, he saw the city recreating itself again. It wasn't just the architecture that appealed to him, it was the city's audacity. Its fearlessness.

Yang added the stamped bank statement to Dorian's file without even looking at it.

"Now we must talk about your Chinese partner." She folded her hands on the desk in front of her expectantly. Dorian managed not to scream.

5.

There had to be other English teachers who didn't really care what they taught, who agreed with Liz that lesson plans were a waste of paper, staff meetings a waste of time. All over Shanghai there were expats who'd been lured by the work visas and the promise that they'd be treated like "pandas": the best housing, food, classes—everything designed to give a good impression. They didn't move to China to make a difference in their students' lives. That was never part of the sales pitch.

Believing she was in the majority made Liz feel better each day, each class period, as she stood outside the various rooms, waiting for the regular first grade teachers to wrap up their lessons and leave, brushing silently past her as they hurried away. On Mondays she had Ms. Rose's class, Ms. Veronica's, and Ms. Mona's all in a row, no free periods in between. She taught more classes than the rest of the first grade teachers, she pointed out often to me, and I was quick to remind her that she taught the same lesson over and over again, whereas the other teachers taught reading, math, history, science. I kept talking and Liz stopped listening, wishing only for some space to complain.

Ms. Rose's students were happy to see her. They always were. They jumped up in their chairs, some of them running up to hug her legs, or pull on her sleeves. Liz wondered often what Ms. Rose did to those poor children.

"Settle, settle," Liz said, and after a few moments they did. She continued to the front of the room, wondering even as she picked up the whiteboard marker what she was going to do that day. Ms. Rose's class was often her first period, her testing ground.

On Mondays things were easier. She wrote MY WEEKEND up on the board and then turned to her students.

"Let's work in pairs," she started, but there was a knock at the door, interrupting her.

"I'm sorry I'm late, dear. Please, continue." Madeline, the head of the English department, entered and waved Liz back up to the front, walking herself toward the far corner of the room. She stood there, holding a clipboard in her hand, squinting at the front of the room, apparently waiting for Liz to continue.

"Oh, okay. Hello, welcome," Liz answered awkwardly. She didn't understand what Madeline was doing there, but from her demeanor it seemed clear that she expected Liz to know.

Liz tried to fake it as best she could, dividing the students into pairs, giving them instructions to discuss what they did over the weekend. They were all talking—in English—Liz kept telling herself. That had to look good. But Madeline kept looking down at her clipboard, squinting, drawing it closer to her face as though it contained microscopic clues that would unlock the meaning of Liz's lesson. *It's just speech class!* Liz wanted to shout as she watched Madeline once again staring up at the board, though the words hadn't changed since she'd entered the room.

Liz had her students switch partners and changed the topic to how they'd celebrated Chinese New Year last month.

"Aren't we going to draw pictures?" one of the boys in the front row asked.

"Not today," Liz whispered, looking quickly to the back of the room to determine if Madeline had heard.

With 15 minutes left, after she'd circled the room enough times to make herself dizzy, checking in on all the conversations going on, she silenced her students and asked them to return to their desks. Thankfully, they did.

"Let's write some sentences on the board together. Sentences you remember from your conversation." This seemed like a good idea, a way to wrap up the lesson in a more formal way. She looked back again, actually expecting a smile. Madeline met her eyes, fierce and confused.

By the time Ms. Rose returned, opening the door unannounced as she always did, Liz was sweating. Ms. Rose began talking to her students while Liz was still mid-sentence. So Liz nodded, hurrying out. Madeline followed her into the hall.

"Thank you. That was—interesting."

"Oh, thanks. Sure. Anytime."

"But I am curious," Madeline continued even as Liz tried to escape down the hallway. "Is this not the lesson you'd submitted for today's class." She thrust her clipboard toward Liz, showing her a lesson with today's date at the top, the lesson I had typed up and submitted for Liz, which I had, as always, offered to Liz for use in the class, which she had, as always, refused.

"I, uh, I decided to switch things around a bit today," she explained. Her voice must have trembled.

"I see. A bit unorthodox for your class observation day."

"Yes, I suppose, but, well, I didn't know you were

coming," Liz shrugged, as though closed the matter.

"But you did receive official notification." It was not a question.

Liz turned the phrase *official notification* over and over in her head, grasping for meaning. The green envelopes, it suddenly occurred to her. The green envelopes she hadn't opened in months. "I did," she rushed. "I did. I'm sorry. I forgot. I haven't been feeling well. I'm very sorry."

Madeline waved her hand back and forth as though it really was just a small thing, and then turned to head back to the office. Liz knew she should tell me what happened, but she didn't want to walk the rest of the way with Madeline and so ducked instead into the staff bathroom a few doors down from her class, locking herself in the far stall, staring down at the toilet in front of her. She waited until it felt safe to come out. Even then she didn't come to my office, though. She didn't know what to say.

6.

Some expats call it a code, communicated via grim smiles and understanding nods as they pass each other on the street—two white faces in the crowd. Because Shanghai can be a confounding place, even for the most prepared. Those who speak the language and understand the culture can still be overcome by exhaustion, by the smells of sweat and smoke and burning rubber assaulting them as vigorously as the noise of jackhammers and the press of bodies surging toward the subway. Sometimes even the little things—the business of living a life—become too much to bear. There is refuge, then, in the upscale restaurants along the Bund, the steam room at the Ritz, the beers at Malone's, where the expats are loud and take up more space than they can generally find anywhere else.

When I first arrived in Shanghai I loved loud expats taking up space. We were outsiders—most of us didn't need Dorian to explain the concept for us to understand—and so we took care of each other. There was safety in numbers.

"Can you check to see if there's a happy hour tonight?" Liz asked as our bus pulled out of the school's driveway one Friday afternoon. She was bored with my hibernating, wanted that other kind of refuge. I hadn't looked at my texts since before lunch, when I'd messaged Liz. But it was Friday; someone had chosen a bar.

She waited as I checked my phone. She never asked me to add her to the group text. Maybe she thought it was impossible. I showed her the message—Zapatas again. I shrugged. "I thought we were going to watch a movie?"

"It would be nice to be around other people a bit," she answered with a smile as she rested her hand on my knee. "We could watch a movie tomorrow?"

"I'm just not feeling that great. But maybe if we stay in tonight and make it an early night, you and I could go out somewhere together tomorrow."

"But happy hour is tonight." She took her hand off my knee and turned to look out the window of the bus. In the shadows of certain buildings, I could see her reflection in the glass, could tell from her expression that she saw it too.

A few minutes later we passed our favorite sculpture. She is a woman, two stories high and silver-bright, her body swan-diving forward, the metal that would have been her legs fused together and forming a backward S with the curve of her torso, arcing like the blade of a wave toward the ground. We pass her every day. In hands extended over her head she holds the two ends of a ribbon; it sails above her, caught in the wind she pushes against. It's a parachute she doesn't need. It wouldn't hold her if she did.

I really wasn't going to go to happy hour. It was already after five when we got home, and Liz hurried into the second bedroom where she still kept her clothes to change. I sat down on the couch and pulled out my phone again, as though re-reading the impersonal message would tell me something. I had a new text from Dorian, sent not to the group but just to me.

Where have you been hiding? I hope you're coming out tonight.

I paused, my fingers hovering over the keyboard. I didn't have to respond. I could turn off my phone, go in my room, and put on pajamas. Liz would tell Dorian I was sick. Liz would get drunk with him, make the faces that she makes. Or if not with Dorian, someone else.

I'll be there, I texted him back.

I called into the other room to tell Liz I'd changed my mind. From the safety of the couch I didn't have to see the disappointment I assume flashed across her face before she came out of her room, still only half clothed.

"Oh good! I'm glad."

I don't know why I didn't believe her, but I assured myself that nothing was falling apart and made myself get dressed.

We drove along Zongshan Road, through the Bund, and Liz admired the architecture, though she didn't know to call it Romanesque, Renaissance, or Baroque. She looked at the brightly lit buildings—no neon there, but warm yellow spotlights, casting their shadows upward, imposing and elegant—and didn't understand their history. She thought of Paris (though she'd never been) as our cab sped down the 10-lane road, unaware that the buildings she gaped at had once housed Europe's banks and trading houses, before the Communist takeover of the country in the 1950s. This city, with its layers and secrets, its histories erased and rewritten, was a perfect place for Liz and me, though she would never understand that in the way I did. A pity. She would have found it interesting that not quite 40 years ago, the Red Guard tried to rewrite the country's history, destroying the religious and cultural artifacts antithetical to the new Communist regime. She would've marveled at the scale of it—millions of people forced to forget!—without stopping to consider each one of those million lives, left in ruin. As it was, she simply stared at the beautiful buildings, noting the way the smog reflected the golden light, seeming to glitter.

I might've explained all this to her, but instead I kept silent. There were histories and histories and histories I never explained to Liz.

She ran her fingers absentmindedly up the side of my leg as she looked out the window. I flinched and pretended not to know what she was hoping would happen when we got to the bar. But I could have written the story that was playing out in her head; I'd lived it already. Not here in Shanghai, not in front of Dorian, but he wasn't really so different from the drunk college boys who watched Alice and me make out at a party, on the crowded dance floor of our favorite bar, in the hallway of our dorm. All those nights were for me a revelation, but for her they were just a game. Everyone has a heart stitched back together, the scars they try to hide.

I shifted in my seat in the back of the cab, making a show of getting comfortable as I pulled my leg out of Liz's reach. Making a show. I couldn't tell yet what I was for Liz: an experiment, a prop, or a person. I was too afraid of what she'd say to ask, too afraid she'd ask me in return what I wanted her to be. Our cab pulled up in front of Zapatas and I emptied my head of the past and the future.

We were late, had missed the crowd that came straight from work for a couple drinks before going home. Dorian was still there, though, seated at a table in the back with a colleague I recognized but whose name I couldn't recall. They were surrounded by empty beer, margaritas, and shot glasses, the detritus of what I hoped was an office gathering that had since dispersed. He stood as we approached and I thought it was for us. But he was craning his neck around the bar, seeming not to notice us at all.

"Where the fuck is our waitress?" he shouted and then he looked at me expectantly, as though he hadn't registered who I was and was instead waiting for me to hand him the drink he'd ordered. The drink he clearly didn't need.

"Sasha!" I'd pulled out a chair before he recognized me. "Have a seat!" He gestured grandly. "I'm happy to see you."

He didn't greet Liz, and though it made me feel petty, I was glad.

I introduced myself to Dorian's friend, though I'd likely met him before. Expats in bars meet each other over and over and over again.

"We were about to do shots," Frank said, after shaking my hand. I let Liz introduce herself so that I didn't have to determine whether to call her my roommate or my girl-friend. She was just Liz; I wanted to drink enough that the naming of things didn't make me anxious. I nodded enthusiastically at Frank's offer and the four of us worked together to flag down the waitress.

"You're just in time for the latest update on my fucking apartment saga. I need a fucking Chinese partner, apparently. Can you believe that shit?" Dorian was at the five-beer level of cursing, at least one per sentence.

Liz slid her chair slightly closer to mine, though it might've appeared she was just aiming for a better angle on the table. Dorian and Frank might not have noticed her finger connecting the dots of the freckles on my forearm before I pulled away to run a hand through my hair. I pursed my lips at her, then looked away.

"So, what? You're just supposed to put an ad in the paper: 'Chinese partner wanted to share condo.' How the fuck do you have a partner in a condo?" Frank asked.

"I have no idea. I tried explaining that to her. It's going to be my fucking house. I'm just supposed to have some Chinese dude living in the spare room? I was nicer than that, I mean, but really, that's the gist."

"Oooh." Frank sat up a little straighter, looking

suddenly excited. "What if you marry a Chinese girl? Can she be your partner?"

I snorted. "You two are being idiots. The partner doesn't live with you."

"You know about this?"

"Our school is all expat families. We help some of them buy. Not many—most of them are set up by their companies—but a few. I've seen the process: it's slow, and—"

"I'm not an idiot," Frank interrupted. "Obviously whoever they assigned wouldn't live there, but if he had a Chinese wife, he wouldn't need the partner. Seriously. This is genius. Whoever you find to marry will be psyched because she gets to live in this sweet condo, right? And brag to her friends about her American husband and his big American dick. She does your laundry and cooks dinners, so you don't have to hire an ayi. Problem solved."

"I'm sorry, you're right. You're not an idiot. You're a complete pig."

I wasn't really kidding, but Frank laughed and took the shot of tequila the waitress had delivered while he'd been laying out his brilliant plan. Meanwhile Dorian turned a deep shade of pink, whether at the mention of big American dicks or at the possibility Frank and I might get into an argument, I couldn't be sure.

"Think about it is all I'm saying." Frank was oblivious to Dorian's embarrassment. "There are no Chinese chicks here, but we can start going to other bars."

"I'll take it under advisement. Meanwhile, my agent said there's an office I can go to, of course. The Office of Foreign Investment. I fill out a bunch of paperwork, and they match me with a Chinese 'investor.' The guy puts his name on the documents with me, and in return I pay him a 'small' monthly fee, whatever that means."

"So…essentially, you have to buy a condo and bring along your own landlord?" Liz asked. I don't know when she'd taken her shot, but her glass was empty. I'd been waiting for the right time to offer a toast, but obviously that moment had passed.

"Essentially. Yes."

"Dude. Why the fuck are you doing this again?"

I wanted to know too.

Dorian shrugged. "The partner doesn't get anything if I sell. Or, maybe he gets a very small percentage. It's still *my* apartment. He has no rights or anything." He looked at me as though for verification. I nodded noncommittally, and took my own shot, ignoring the lime sitting beside my glass. The tequila was all heat and smoke on the back of my throat. I wanted another.

I signaled the waitress while Frank groaned and pushed away from the table. As he left he wished Dorian luck and mumbled something about it being good to meet Liz. He was snubbing me, or he was drunker than he seemed. I didn't really care.

We did another round of tequila, this time all together after a chorus of *gan bei*. Heat rose in my chest, and the bar seemed smaller.

Liz sounded annoyed as she asked where the bathroom was, as though she had to repeat the question, as though I'd kept her waiting. Maybe I had.

After I directed her to the back of the bar, she made more noise than necessary getting up and I both loved and feared her for her moodiness, her drama.

Dorian didn't look up as she stood, and instead moved his chair closer to mine. I was hemmed in from either side. I leaned away from him, too imperceptibly for him to notice.

"When are we having dinner?"

"It sounds like you're going to have your nights occupied by your search for a Chinese bride." I meant it as a joke, but Dorian's eyes narrowed. Rather than blushing his skin blanched.

"Frank is an asshole," he said quietly. "You should

know I would never even consider something like that."

I laughed and waved my hands at him, treating the serious mood he'd fallen into like a cloud of cigarette smoke I could disperse without inhaling. I needed another drink, opted for a margarita—something to keep my hands and mouth busy for longer than just one shot. Liz was still in the bathroom, so I ordered one for her too.

"Let me take you out. I need your advice about the apartment."

He reached forward and rested his pointer finger on my knee.

"I really don't have any advice for you," I told him, tensing up and leaning back even farther in my chair. He didn't move his hand. I don't know why I didn't make him.

I wasn't entirely sure what was going on. I could list, if not by name then at least by sight, a large portion of the women Dorian had fucked over the years, or at least the women he went home with; I couldn't say what happened once they left the bars where Dorian had plied them with martinis or margaritas or sake bombs.

He tended to favor tall, willowy types, usually blonde. Not quite models, but the kind of girls who'd been told by their various aunts and their more jealous friends that they could be models, girls who smiled and thought briefly about it, but who secretly feared they were too plain, too chubby, too short, too tall. These girls flocked to Shanghai, though they didn't belong: they came on a semester abroad or were passing through on their way to Thailand or Laos or India. Maybe that's what attracted him: their impermanence.

Three years earlier, had I been asked to look around my circle of expat acquaintances and choose the ones who would still be there so many happy hours later, I wouldn't have picked Dorian. If his women were flighty, temporary, Dorian had always struck me as a bit too serious for China. And though he tried to appear confident, he always looked to me to be a bit unsure, confused, as though he'd been roped into playing a game whose rules he didn't completely understand.

"Advice about what?" The question arrived at the table before Liz did.

"Condos," I answered loudly, finally shifting enough in my seat that my leg was out of Dorian's casual reach, though not before Liz's gaze landed on his hand on my knee. "I ordered you a margarita," I rushed. "I hope that's okay."

She looked sideways at the two of us as she sat. I had nothing to hide from her, but still I felt guilty.

Drinks with straws are a balm to my anxiety, the plastic providing the perfect level of resistance for the nervous workings of my jaw. Imagine chewing frantically on a bright red coffee stirrer while your girlfriend fights with your father. She yelled so loud I might have tufted out of there on a sound wave, had I been ready.

7.

I slid close to Liz in the back of the cab on the way home, but the space I'd created between us didn't get any smaller.

"That was fun." Liz said sarcastically.

"You're upset." As though she needed me to tell her.

"No, I loved spending the night watching a good-looking guy hit on my girlfriend while I'm being ignored."

"I wasn't ignoring you."

She turned away from me to stare out the window. Looking back, I wonder if it was my attention she'd been missing. At the time I thought I was getting the silent treatment I deserved.

"I'm sorry," I said to the back of Liz's head. "I don't know why this is so hard for me." It would have been closer to the truth to say I didn't know how to explain to her why it was hard, but even that seemed like saying too much. I willed the traffic to disperse and our cab to speed up, wanting the safety of our apartment.

"I know this is new for us, but really—I don't understand why you are so secretive about it. There's nothing to be ashamed of."

Histories and histories and histories.

"I know that. I'm not ashamed."

"Then what is it? You can't expect me to just accept that you don't know."

Our cab pulled into the semi-circular driveway in front of our building. I paid the fare—the least I could do—counting the bills slowly, buying time.

Alice had turned us into a spectacle. I was complicit—reliant on alcohol and dim party lights to push me through my inexperience, and to drown out the questions I didn't know yet how to answer. But my feelings for her were real. The titillated onlookers were never the point.

Was Liz an Alice or a Heather? It scared me that I couldn't tell.

"I just need some more time to feel settled, and less anxious. It's only been a couple of months. I'm still trying to get used to this," is what I said.

It was the right thing to say to earn her sympathy.

"Only that long? God, it feels like so much longer, don't you think? I feel like we've been together forever."

"Well, it has been longer since you moved in. Maybe that's really when it all started."

Liz laughed. "Like I was some mail-order-bride you sent for from America."

I bit my lip. "Actually," I answered slowly, "I did send for you." A minor secret, something I thought I could give her.

"What do you mean?"

"I found you. I brought you here. I gave your résumé to the principal. He didn't look at any other applicants. Actually," I paused and chuckled at this, "I told him there were no other applicants."

"What? Why?"

"I just had a sense, I guess. I don't really know, exactly.

It was the e-mail you sent, I think. I just knew you needed to be here."

I liked to imagine Liz writing her cover letter. From the time stamp I knew it had been the middle of the night, and so I pictured her in a dark apartment, her hair in a messy bun, her eyes red—strained from too long in front of a glowing computer screen and maybe the desperate tears of someone who needed an escape.

As a job application, the materials she sent were terrible—and they weren't the versions I eventually gave to the principal—but they were enough to win me over.

She stepped into the elevator ahead of me without answering and crossed her arms over her chest, keeping her gaze on the floor.

"Are you mad?" This time I was surprised.

"I don't know."

"It was fate, Liz. Fate."

She didn't answer, and the doors to the elevator slid closed in front of us.

"What did you see?"

"What do you mean?"

"What did you see in me? What made you want to bring me here?"

"You signed the letter 'Besottedly.'" That wasn't really it, or wasn't all of it, but it was all I could give her.

Liz shrugged. "It means drunk."

I shook my head. "It means in love."

8.

"I have something to tell you."

We were getting ready for bed, brushing our teeth beside each other, talking through the foam—the way roommates do rather than lovers. Not because of my hesitancy with her that evening, or even because she knew I'd manipulated her hiring. It was just how we were some nights. I didn't mind that things between us weren't always romantic, or that we didn't have as much sex as we could've. There was comfort in it. It made me feel safe.

Though now she spoke without making eye contact in the mirror and my anxiety spiked.

"Madeline came to observe my class today."

I exhaled loudly at the mention of work. Things with us were fine. We were fine.

"I think it went really badly."

"Badly how?"

"Well, the lesson I taught didn't match the plan she had."

I closed my eyes and inhaled, kept them closed as

I asked, "Why didn't they match?" I spoke slowly in an attempt to convey calm, though I think it had the opposite effect, at least on me.

"I didn't know she was coming." She said it softly, but there was an indignant edge to her voice. She didn't want to have to explain herself to me. But now that she understood the role I had in hiring, she realized she had to.

The fight we had next about one thing that couldn't be changed was so much worse than the one we had in the cab about many things still left undone.

I didn't know if I was more upset that she hadn't been opening any of the green envelopes, or that she hadn't been using any of the lesson plans I'd risked my job to give her.

I asked about the envelopes first, trying to remember as I did what other school announcements or requirements I'd opted to convey via proverb.

"You told me not to worry about them!"

"I told you not to worry about the ones with due dates for lesson plans. I didn't say to stop opening them."

"Why does it even matter? I just want to figure out what to do about this terrible observation. Can I get a do-over or something? Am I in trouble because my lesson didn't match the plans?"

I pinched the bridge of my nose, shaking my head and staring down at the bathroom floor.

I blamed myself, but I wasn't about to tell Liz that. I'd gotten distracted, had assumed that Liz's silence regarding the envelopes meant she had everything under control. I've learned since then not to make assumptions about silence.

I offered Liz none of this generosity. "I still don't understand why you haven't been using the lessons I've been handing in. It makes absolutely no sense."

"I know." She was working hard not to cry. "You never should've given me this job."

"You can do this."

Liz started to laugh. "Right. I can do it. I'm just the worst speech teacher in the history of this school."

I didn't answer.

"It's fine. I know I'm terrible. But you know, you're the one who brought me here. You're the one who thought I could do it. Now I'm probably going to get fired. What do we do?" She was ready to hear the alternatives. I would help her find a new job, or I would tell her that maybe she could take some time off, just a little while.

"You're not going to get fired. Not during the school year."

Liz sighed. "How do you know?"

"Well, the principal hasn't asked me to put out a new job listing, so there's no one to replace you. At least not yet. You still have time to improve."

I wanted her to nod, full of hope and the resolve to become a better teacher. The best she could do, though, was to blink her eyes slowly.

"We'll figure it out," I promised, reaching for her hand as I turned to leave the bathroom, pulling her along behind me. "Don't worry."

WE WISH FOR STARS

気

I wish I were a stronger person: the kind who packs away a wooden box containing the tokens of a failed relationship without opening it, or the kind who just throws it away; the kind who says goodbye without cutting open all the wounds that have only just begun to heal. The kind who closes the fucking computer.

In her wedding photos Liz looks older. It's not just that she's married—children do that all the time. There's something in her eyes now: something more than the glisten of tears as she stands under a tree in her wedding gown, holding her husband's two hands in her own. Am I surprised she married a man? I search the hollows of my heart, my gut.

In another photo Liz and her groom hold glasses of champagne, the edge of hers already smeared with cranberry lipstick. She's smiling, looking off to the side at someone outside the frame.

So many of her albums are public. After the reception and the ceremony, I admire the French manicure, and the sassy grin peeking out from a curtain of half-done hair. She's holding champagne in that one too, the manicure and the engagement ring framed for the camera by the fluted glass. More bubbly at brunch, the bride-to-be in a crisp white shirt-dress—button-down for easy removal.

I assume it's her mother who buttons up the back of her wedding gown. An older man who loves Liz and loves the woman I assume is her mother stands in front of them both, tears in his eyes. A father full of pride.

She had an amazing photographer.

In another picture they stand in profile framed by a doorway. Standing behind her, Liz's father is wearing a vest but no jacket, a pale pink tie. He fastens the clasp of her necklace. The single strand of pearls ripples over her collarbone like water.

Resting a hand on the strand still around my own neck, I look back at the pictures of the ceremony, wondering how I could've missed it.

1.

Shanghai is always rushing, or it doesn't move at all. Cars careen through intersections and down narrow streets, barely missing pedestrians, bikes, and mopeds; or traffic creeps, forming millipedes of headlights stretching in all directions from the city's center to its edges. Construction projects race toward completion, the steel skeletons of new skyscrapers welded by workers who sleep on site and work round-the-clock shifts, until one day the workers are gone, banished by bureaucrats. The hollow buildings they leave behind are the city's broken promises.

Raised in Shanghai, Sam should have felt this push and pull in his blood. He couldn't match the city's rhythms though: hurried when he should have meandered, stood still when he should have leapt.

Or he got on the bus, sighing and pulling at his collar to make more room to breathe. The grime of the city mixed with the grime of the passengers and the weight of their days carried in heavy plastic bags; the air smelled of gasoline and sweat and fish. The floor vibrated beneath

Sam's feet as the bus lurched away from the curb.

He took a deep breath—through his mouth—and counted silently to ten. His phone buzzed. After several attempts at shifting his bag from one shoulder to the other, widening his stance to steady himself on the rocking bus, disrupting and in two cases elbowing the other passengers who crowded around him, he was able to remove the phone from his snug pocket.

He read the text from Li Qin: a knife-sharp reminder that Sam should bring a date to Li Qin's birthday party, a repeated offer to bring a woman for Sam if he couldn't find his own. Everyone Sam knew was looking for a wife, using bottles of vodka and tables in the dark corners of nightclubs, shined shoes and silver watches, cell phones and stereos, new cars and gold fixtures like bait—all of it different from the rest of the flashing lights in Shanghai, but the same.

The bus pulled up at his stop and Sam forced his way to the door, exhaling in relief as the wall of flesh crammed inside expelled him onto the sidewalk. He headed away from Jiujiang Road to the tea lounge he and Liz decided to try. He'd finally given in to her requests. But he wasn't going in without her.

She was almost 20 minutes late. For the first time since they started meeting, Sam thought about giving up. That was his nerves, though, and he made himself stay still. Finally, he saw her turn the corner at the end of the road. It was relief he felt. Or it was dread.

She looked surprised to see him standing outside. "I'm so sorry! I had some trouble finding it. Are they closed?"

"No, no." Sam shook his head and ushered her through the door. "*Ni hao*," he mumbled to the staff as they entered. The tea house was, as he feared, completely empty. The waitresses tittered and rushed to bring them water and menus. Keeping with the Chinese custom, she placed the menus on the table and then stood immediately beside them, waiting for their order. A second server hovered just a few feet away, as though there might be a tea emergency that required her assistance.

Sam fought the urge to groan, speaking quickly to them instead, ordering for himself and Liz just to get them to go away.

"So…" he turned back to Liz.

"My first real tea house!" she cut him off. She looked around excitedly, at the rough wooden tables and chairs, the heavy drapes, the fake flowers carefully arranged in the corners. Seven months in China and she hadn't yet been inside a tea house. Sam assumed she'd been waiting for him to take her.

They talked about work, as they often did, and Sam began to feel calmer.

"I'm worried I might be fired," Liz admitted, wrapping one hand around her cup of unidentified tea; Sam knew what he'd ordered for them of course, but Liz didn't ask, and he didn't feel compelled to volunteer the information.

He assumed she wanted him to comfort her, and so he reached across the table and rested his hand atop hers, just briefly, the way a friend might.

"Would your girlfriend let that happen?"

"I'm not sure Sasha can help."

"Don't be silly." His voice was steady, and he wondered if he should reach his hand toward her once more. "Who would right now be looking for your replacement if you were going to be fired?"

Liz shrugged, appearing younger than she really was. "I suppose that's true."

"It's certainly true. Just talk to her and see."

There was a pause as they sipped their tea.

"And if your job is in danger, please let me know. I could perhaps help you find a new one, at one of the schools where I work. Maybe even a better job than talking to first graders." Because Sam had heard her complaints about the work. He'd been listening and making plans.

"That's so nice of you. Thank you."

Sam nodded. "I'm your friend, you know?"

Liz wasn't very good at making eye contact, but if she held it for a moment you could see the flecks of gold in her brown eyes. "Yes," she said. "I know."

She didn't have friends. Not really. There was the girl next door when she was 11. They spent six weeks during the summer before fifth grade practicing kissing through their t-shirts; wearing two halves of the same silver necklace; playing hopscotch with no shoes on, the soles of their feet turning blue from the chalk. But when school started the girl had looked through Liz as though she didn't know her.

In junior high, Liz was always invited to all the things the whole class was invited to. Later she was invited to all the things Bryan was invited to. Everyone knew her name, but were they her friends? Liz never thought so.

"I have a favor to ask of you, too."

"Of course!" she answered, because she felt indebted.

"I need a date. To my friend Li Qin's birthday party."

Liz made thinking noises and then listed for Sam the expats she knew who might want to be set up. There weren't many options, but surely someone would be available.

"I'm sorry," Sam interrupted her. "I wasn't clear. I was hoping you would come with me to the party."

"Oh... I..."

"I know you are with Sasha," he rushed. "I just need a friend who can pretend. Li Qin has someone he'd like me to take, and my mother also knows a girl..."

"But you don't want to go with either of them," Liz finished for him.

He nodded, relieved he didn't have to say it.

"I can be your pretend date."

It didn't occur her to ask why he didn't find a real date

he did want to take. She was flattered, and she wanted to go.

But she waited too long to tell me.

2.

Expats in China are used to waiting. They wait in consulates for visas; at police stations to register their addresses; at the medical offices for their exams; at the banks to open accounts, deposit into accounts, withdraw from accounts, or for the forms required to prove they had accounts; they wait in lines at local convenience stores to pay their utility bills, and in the grocery stores to check their bags; they wait for subways and busses and taxis. Everywhere they are waiting for taxis.

Dorian was waiting, too. For a while, he thought about the apartment everyday: scouted neighborhoods, imagined the most preferable floor plans, perused the interior design magazines scattered around his office, debated the question of ordering furniture from abroad (extravagant) versus buying in China (risky). After a couple of months of this, however, he'd begun to feel ridiculous, like a cat on a leash, controlled by Shanghai bureaucracy. Or like one of those small dogs he saw being pushed in strollers all over the city; most of the time they were wearing dresses.

He knew he was taking the whole thing too personally. There were no bureaucrats sitting around some smoke-filled conference room talking about him. *"Should we give the American his foreign investor today?"* Much laughter. *"I heard he's starting to look at carpet samples."* More laughter. *"Let's let him dangle a little longer."* It wasn't happening, he knew. He wasn't the protagonist in a Kafka novel. But sometimes he just wondered.

Finally, he received a letter notifying him of his time to appear at the Office of Foreign Investment. Once he arrived, though he had the appointment, he waited in a line that at first glance seemed quite short but turned out to be interminably unmoving.

The other four people in line were all men, all white. They didn't make eye contact with each other—no shared sigh, shrug, or eye roll; Dorian was used to instant camaraderie amongst *lǎowài*; he didn't know how to handle this silence.

They were older than Dorian, had likely been to the office before, conducting the kind of "important" business Dorian's brother would approve of. Ah, Simon. Dorian chuckled to himself at the thought of his brother standing in this line. But no. Simon would never have made it to this line. Simon would've given up at the wait for the appointment, or perhaps even earlier: the official stamp on the bank record, or the Bureau of Employment Verification. For all his talk of seizing days, of early birds and worms, Dorian knew that Simon opted always for the well-paved road. His success depended on the work of others. It had been true since high school. He was student council president thanks to his campaign manager girlfriend; he floated through honors classes thanks to the study groups he charmed his way into.

It used to make Dorian jealous, but he'd come to see it as a major character flaw. He would rather have patience and perseverance than luck and charm. But then, Dorian did have charm. At least some people thought so—his co-workers, for example, and sometimes his dates. I apparently didn't think he had any, but he was trying to put that behind him. He must've been waiting to run into me again so he could demonstrate just how far behind him it was.

He was finally called into an inner office—after the other four more important-looking men in line—and he knew immediately from the bare, dingy walls, the smaller than normal desk, the man's uniform, that this was a bullshit meeting with a low-level functionary. The man was smoking a cigarette, tapping ash periodically into an already brimming ashtray. His hair hung down in his eyes and his jowls hung below his chin. He gestured to the seat opposite his desk, and when Dorian sat, he nodded and slid a form over. It was all basic information, everything that was included in his file with Yang Xue and submitted along with his request for this appointment: name, occupation, passport number, date of visa, income, bank account number. The man leaned forward in his seat, pushing himself halfway out of his chair and dangling his cigarette precariously between his lips, attempting to read Dorian's answers as he wrote. When Dorian finished, he slid the form back across the desk and was informed that the agency would contact him.

"When?" Dorian asked.

The man raised his palms to the ceiling.

Dorian prepared to wait some more.

Not knowing how long he'd be trapped in this purgatory of paperwork, Dorian decided thinking about the apartment was too depressing, and he tried to stop. Not thinking about the apartment, it turned out, was equally depressing: his life, he realized, was empty. Forget the question of whether a new apartment—carpets and tile and stainless steel appliances, sleek modern furniture, high thread-count sheets—could ever fill such a void. He just needed something to tide him over.

Which is how he found himself at Blue Frog, holding a martini glass the size of a toaster oven. Dorian stared down at his nearly empty drink, contemplating what to do next. He hadn't been back to Blue Frog in a long time. It was near the Xujiahui Mall, another place he didn't go anymore. With all its high-end stores—Guess, Marc Jacobs, and the like—the mall felt entirely too American to Dorian, too much like Pioneer Square back home in Portland, where his mother met her friends for afternoons of lunch and shopping.

He groaned and pulled out his phone, in need of a distraction. Where have you been? he tapped. The Blue Frog misses you. He set the phone down on his leg and waited for my response, turning to face the rest of the bar and leaning his back against his table. Half the people in the bar, he guessed, were trying to text their way out of their current situations, looking for any available options.

That's how expats are.

No one ever goes to a place just to be there. Each bar is a stopover until the next text comes in, the next taxi pulls up out front. At the next bar—wherever it is—there'll be smaller crowds, or bigger ones, cheaper drinks, or better ones. There'll be something you don't even know you're looking for, or someone looking for you.

Dorian didn't know if it was the same in American bars. Before China he'd lived in Seattle, working for the same firm he did now, talking to anyone who would listen about being transferred to the Shanghai office. Always at his best when focused on achieving a goal, he worked late and spent much of his free time keeping up on his Mandarin. He didn't go to bars much. He didn't like feeling adrift.

Now he had no choice. He'd met up with some people from the office, but they'd long since scattered around the bar, or followed their text leads to other locales. One girl, new in the office (and to the country) had lingered around Dorian for a bit, tossing her hair and occasionally touching his arm, sipping her drink in a way he understood was supposed to look sexy but came off forced, somewhat desperate. Dorian contemplated, briefly, playing a game: *How Horribly Will You Allow Me to Behave?* For example, could he get her to pay for his drinks? Could he get her to pay for his drinks and then give him a blow job in the bathroom? Could he take the blow job and then put her in a cab home by herself?

In college, Dorian—like most of his friends—had been inadvertently horrible to women. At first he didn't realize what he was doing. Once he learned, he'd turned it into a game, seeing how far he could go. He assumed that at least half the time he'd be slapped in the face, and he accepted that. But it never happened. Eventually he saw there was no point to a game he couldn't lose. He contemplated playing tonight out of boredom, but then imagined the awkwardness in the office on Monday and thought better of it. He really was growing up.

Of course, *not* trying to get the blow job in the bathroom made it increasingly likely that it would happen. The girl was hard to get rid of, but eventually he'd told her that his good friend John—"you know John, the quiet guy with the cube in the corner"—was desperately in love with her, and Dorian just wouldn't forgive himself if something happened between them. She'd looked at him sweetly, kissed him full on the mouth like they were both saying goodbye to something wonderful that could never be, and left. Dorian guessed from the kiss that she'd give a lousy blow job. He'd ordered another martini. That was an hour ago.

His phone buzzed to life. Is that some nickname for your penis? If so, not sexy. Also, inaccurate, as of course you know "the blue frog" and I have never met.

Dorian laughed out loud and rubbed his chin, trying

to formulate a response. The reason he'd never lost the *How Horrible* game was that he'd never played it with someone like me.

You know I can always arrange an introduction, he typed, and then pictured me rolling my eyes and tossing my phone to the side of my bed. He quickly revised. How crass! I was simply inviting you out for a drink. Send.

It's a little late for invitations out on a Friday night, isn't it? Do you think I'm just sitting around in my fancy pants, waiting for a gentleman caller?

Dorian looked around the bar, smiling, wishing momentarily for someone toward whom he could tip his phone. But then, no. He wanted it just to himself.

I recognize you and your fancy pants must have many other offers. But then, you are free to answer text messages…

It's intermission at the opera.

A perfect time to cut and run!

My date would be so disappointed.

He's probably wearing fancy pants himself. Ditch him, I say.

I heard the water turn off in Liz's shower and set my phone down, waiting for her to come in the bedroom, cocooned in her fuzzy bathrobe, smelling like jasmine shampoo. I debated telling her about Dorian: *He's flirting with me, look. It's hilarious.* I wondered, briefly, what jealousy might add to the relationship stew I'd been simmering, allowing to thicken: a hint of spice, perhaps, or too much bitterness? *Don't worry*, I could have said. *It's all because of you. He only wants me now because I'm in love. I'm glowing and he can sense it.*

Heather had made me sparkle, silver-white and hot, a supergiant star. My father noticed the glow and did what he could to make sure no one else ever saw it. His jaw got tighter and tighter in the days after he'd seen the two of us naked and entangled. I was mortified, but Heather had been set free. She kissed me whenever she wanted after that, whether my father was around or not. I was living with him that summer, while she and I made plans, and it seemed he was always around. And if not him, then people he knew. Life in a small town.

I was resolved to ignore his pleas for discretion, but they sent Heather over the edge. At first, I was flattered that she was fighting him on my behalf, until I realized she was fighting for herself. She'd had enough of my cowering but wasn't going to leave quietly. I was surprised at how quickly my light and heat faded after she'd gone. I was a moon, I realized, just reflecting her.

It was different with Liz. I pictured my aura as I re-read Dorian's texts—soft and pillowy, like cotton candy. Gold, with a slightly pink shimmer. It kept me warm and gave me goose bumps. Liz came into the room, damp and fluffy, the living embodiment of my love glow. I stared at her, squinting. I wanted to kiss her.

"I should get in the shower," I said instead, distracting myself from thoughts of my aura out of fear I would accidentally tell Liz that I loved her. Because I wouldn't be the one to say it first.

"What are you up to tonight?" she was pulling tank tops out of her closet, trying one on and then another.

I stopped halfway through undressing. "I thought I was going to Guandii with you."

"Oh." She paused and looked at me. "I didn't…I mean, I thought…"

I cocked my head. "Unless…I'm not invited?" It was obvious I wasn't, but I phrased it as a question anyway.

"It's not really my place to invite you," she answered finally. "I mean, it's Sam's friend's party."

"Right. Of course. Sam's friend's exclusive, invitation-only gathering in the corner of a public nightclub."

"It's not that. It's just…I mean—"

"Stop saying 'I mean,'" I interrupted, "unless you're

going to say what you actually mean."

"Fine. Sam asked me to be his date."

"His date?"

"Not like a *real* date," she rushed to add.

"You're going on a date?"

"Will you just listen?" she snapped. "Li Qin keeps trying to set Sam up, and he didn't want to deal with it. He asked me to come as a pretend date, just to shut his friends up."

Suddenly aware that I was still half-naked, I pulled my t-shirt back over my head. "So does a pretend date put out at the end of the night?"

She glared at me and then turned and left the bedroom. A moment later I heard the blow dryer turn on. I crawled into bed and pulled the covers up over my head. I couldn't tell if I was being mean, or if she was.

"I'm sorry I didn't make this clear earlier," she burst in talking loudly. She'd amped herself up in the bathroom, had worked out all her arguments. "I should have explained. I'm sorry you were expecting to come. Sam asked me as a friend. I'm trying to be a good friend."

"It's fine," I answered from underneath the covers. I didn't know how to take apologies, but then it didn't sound like she was sorry.

"I hope you have an okay night." She'd finished getting ready and leaned down to kiss me goodbye. She'd gone with wide leg jeans fitted tightly across her butt, a short sleeve light blue top, and, to my surprise, her pearls.

"You're wearing pearls to Guandii?" I sat up in bed, her bad fashion choices apparently enough to make me forget my anger.

She turned away from me to look in the mirror. "What? It's kind of a retro look." She shrugged, and then smiled at me.

"But Elizabeth. The wedding day pearls—at a night-club? What would your mother say if she saw you now?"

It was easier to pretend I wasn't hurt.

"I think she'd have more questions about the woman I'm sharing a bed with than the pearls I'm wearing out." She landed the kiss she'd intended earlier and then straightened up, smoothing her shirt. "I'll see you later."

"Have fun," I said. I didn't mean it.

She closed the door behind her and I felt like a child who'd been tucked in for the night, left with the nurse while Mummy in her pearls went out.

I reached for my phone, intending to bring it out into the living room with me and put on a movie. The conversation with Dorian was still up on the screen. I did think before I texted, but not for very long.

Opera's over. Want to hang out?

Forty minutes earlier, I would've been confident of a quick response from Dorian, but who knows what he was doing then. Texting makes real conversation impossible. Forty minutes before, he was likely waiting for some biting response to his suggestion that I ditch my date. How long did he keep his phone in his hand before sighing and setting it down? Was it on the table next to him or in his pocket? Or had he even noticed the delay? I was perhaps one of many possibilities for Dorian that night. I chose a movie—*Ocean's Eleven*. I found the scant dialogue, Vegas jazz, and tones of gold and burgundy soothing. I couldn't just sit next to my phone all night.

Was Mr. Fancy Pants that disappointing?

Danny Ocean had just gotten out of prison. It was a strange amount of time to have passed for Dorian's response: too short if he'd moved on with his evening, too long if he'd still been hoping to hear from me. Just long enough, though, for him to overthink his reply.

I could spend all night engaged in the banter, texting with Dorian until Liz stumbled home, or didn't. But I didn't want to banter.

Meet me in an hour?

3.

Shanghai glittered at night, a sparkle you stopped noticing if you lived here long enough. Or you understood that it was only the tiny particles of smog and soot in the air, refracting the neon light.

Liz knew Guandii the way we went to Guandii: fretting about the cover and ordering the strongest cheapest drinks we could: shots of Jäger, cheap tequila, well vodka on ice. It wasn't that we couldn't afford to be there, but we both liked the narrative of living cheaply in China. Plus we went to Guandii a lot.

Li Qin paid for the bottle service. Top shelf vodka and a pitcher of green tea as a mixer, a tower of pint glasses atop the table. The table—the whole point. The ones in the back of Guandii were like a miniature version of the Shanghai real estate market. You paid for your location.

They weren't hard to spot: five Chinese men being loud, two women and a Chinese man who turned out to be Sam sitting in the corner, talking seriously, and Liz, the only American, standing with a straw in her mouth slurping at her drink. That sounds like a cliché or an insult, but I thought she looked amazing.

Not hard to spot if you were looking, but Dorian didn't notice them. "Let's get a drink." I spoke close to his ear to be heard over the bass. But he was already moving in that direction, tugging on my fingers to follow.

We drank shots of Jägermeister, the bottles hanging from the back of the bar like bats.

Sam asked Liz to dance. Or she asked him. Who can hear anything in that place? The point is they were dancing and I saw them. I finished my second shot. When I ordered three more, Dorian was either intrigued or impressed, then deflated when I handed one to him and walked away from the bar.

"I just saw Liz," I explained as though it was all just a big coincidence. "I'll be right back."

The alcohol had made me brave. I tapped on her shoulder, trying to ignore Sam's hand on her waist, and when she turned I handed her the shot, a fake smile attempting to mask the accusatory raise of my eyebrows.

"Turns out this is a public club and not a private party," I said.

"Sasha," she answered slowly, sounding confused rather than angry. "What are you doing here?"

"Dorian invited me. He's here with some people." I gestured vaguely over my shoulder to the crowds at the bar, any number of whom might have been Dorian's friends. None of them were, but that wasn't the point. I leaned past her before she could answer. "I'm Sasha," I said to Sam, offering my hand.

"I've heard so much about you," he answered, bending toward me and shouting into my ear.

"I'm glad." I smiled, unsure myself whether I was trying to be friendly or somehow intimidating. "Anyway, I just came over to say hi. I'll leave you two to your party." I kissed my shot glass against Liz's, as though a forced toast would convey that things between us were just fine. She stared at me while I drank my shot, her own hand unmoving.

"Give it to the birthday boy if you don't want it." I shrugged as though I didn't care and left the dance floor. She followed me, but not immediately.

I felt her hand on my shoulder before I heard her voice. "Was coming here really necessary, Sasha?"

Echoes of my father. "Was running away in the middle of the night really necessary, Sasha?" His voice, crossing half the globe to reach me, crackled. Or it was just the sound of disappointment.

I was being overly dramatic, but it was my way and I didn't care.

"Is there some kind of fun my presence is preventing you from having?"

A night club is a good place to have a fight. Liz shouted at me and no one noticed. "You're the one who showed up here with a guy who spends all his time hitting on you! What does Dorian think you're doing here? I know you didn't tell him you came for me."

"Don't be stupid," I said. "I didn't come for you."

"Why *did* we come?"

I hadn't seen Dorian approach, but there he was, handing us each another shot. I noticed for the first time that Liz didn't have the one I'd given her. She'd given it to Sam. His drinks distributed, Dorian rested his hand on my waist. Liz's gaze followed it there.

"Obviously some place where you could be alone would be better."

My mouth opened then closed. Dorian looked as though he was about to thank Liz for the helpful suggestion.

The first time, only time, I tried to kiss Alice when we were alone—in my dorm room getting ready for a party—she giggled and asked me what I was doing.

"I'm kissing you."

"I know. But…why?"

I could think of too many ways to answer that. None of them were right, I'm sure, but the one I chose was most wrong.

Alice left because she believed me when I told her I loved her; Heather because she didn't.

Love was skittish. Love was skeptical.

My father was wrong. I hadn't run away to Shanghai in the middle of the night. The move took months of planning. True, I'd packed my bags after he and my stepmother had gone to sleep, had left a note on the kitchen counter, and stepped silently out of the house at 4:15 a.m. when the headlights of my cab had illuminated the darkened driveway. But that was just what time I needed to leave to catch my flight. I walked calmly to the curb. I never ran.

It was the only thing I could think to do after he'd driven away my girlfriend with all his talk about how he didn't care about what kind of *lifestyle* I chose, but he was worried what other people might think. He was only thinking of me. My future.

When I called him from the airport in Shanghai I told him not to bother coming after me. There was a long pause while I prepared for what was coming next. *Who do you think you are and what do you think you're doing and you don't just get to…whose money do you think it is anyway…you're not prepared to deal with this and you need to come home you need to come home you need to come home.* Home. I would laugh. I would tell my father just how little he understood about that word. That would be the end.

But instead of reciting the lines I'd scripted for him in my head, my father had sighed. "Please don't be so dramatic. Nobody's coming after you. You're an adult, Sasha. If you want to live in China, I can't stop you. I know you weren't happy here. I hope you're happy there. I hope you're taking care of yourself."

"Okay," I'd sputtered.

"Do you have a job? A place to live?"

"Yes." My last chance to lie to him.

"Good. Please stay in touch. And keep the credit card for emergencies."

Keep the credit card—my father's idea of "I love you."

I didn't want to fight with Liz. I wanted to be home in bed with her, curled around each other like a set of commas, each of us a pause for the other one to breathe through. Or I wanted to be home alone watching *Ocean's Eleven*, waiting for her to come back to me. Instead I was here on the edge of a crowded dance floor. The music was loud, the lights dizzying. I took the shot Dorian handed me because what else was I supposed to do with it? Liz took hers so she could cross her arms over her chest and glare at me. Sam stood beside her with no shot, his hands in his pockets.

"I'm sorry," I whispered.

Her face softened and she brought her hand to my cheek, touching it lightly with her forefinger, middle finger, holding her thumb on my jawline. Dorian watched us. Dorian saw.

I kissed her. I couldn't think of anything else to do.

Love is skittish. Love is skeptical.

When we parted she tipped her forehead down again, resting it against my own.

I closed my eyes. Sam watched us, and so did his friends. They all saw. I kissed her again.

She reached behind her neck then and unclasped the necklace that—she'd been right—looked somehow more stylish than pearls should've in a night club. Putting her arms around my neck, she fastened the clasp without needing to look.

"I love you," she said, and I sucked in a breath in a panic, afraid the words had come from me. But Liz was soft and open and looking at me.

"I love you, too," I answered. Our voices were hushed, but not because it was a secret.

4.

I pulled her to dance. Her smile was broad, a funhouse mirror reflection of my own nervous grin. I kept my eyes down as I wrapped my arms around her waist and pressed my nose into her collarbone. Our hips drew closer, moving in time to the music, and I pretended I didn't know we were being watched—by Dorian, by Sam and his friends, the other small clusters of strangers around the dance floor. Women danced together all the time in clubs, but not like this. Liz kissed me again and I breathed my anxiety into her open mouth.

The song ended. "Let's get a drink," she suggested. I turned toward the bar, preparing myself to meet Dorian's eye, to answer with the crease in my eyebrows and a firm jut of my lip whatever questions he had. But he wasn't looking at us. He was leaning, elbow up on the bar, talking to two Western men. I'd lied about him having friends here, but it turned out to be true.

Liz tugged at my sleeve. "We have drinks at the table. Come talk to Sam. I want you to get to know him."

Sam and his friends watched us approach. There were the ones who were smirking, the ones who were looking at the ground, and Sam, who was doing neither but was instead looking at Liz, or just beyond her head, his lips pursed and his head cocked as though he were solving complicated equations.

Liz, a better date than friend, handed me a drink. Her hand left my glass and traveled up my arm, caressing my shoulder. I forced myself not to flinch, reminding myself these smirking men were nothing to me. But to Liz, Sam was someone. Was she ignoring the defiant cross of his arms, the blush creeping up his neck? Or did she not notice?

Liz reached past me with another pint glass of vodka and green tea, as though it was her party to host, a wide smirk on her face. Dorian reached out, a surprised recipient of Liz's generosity.

"So…" he rocked on his heels and took a long sip of his drink, holding the straw Liz had given him against the back of glass and letting the ice cubes rest on his top lip as he sipped. "You ladies having fun?"

Are you ladies going out? I heard my father ask.

But Liz laughed. "Great time. You?"

Dorian's face told me he'd been expecting me to answer, but my attention was split in too many different ways, Dorian's only one of a handful of voices in my head. Underneath all of them was my father's, speaking disappointment. Loudest at that moment, though, were Sam's friends.

"You didn't tell us your date was a *lala*, Sam," Li Qin said. He thought speaking Mandarin kept him safe from the *lǎowài*.

I came close to asking him whether we were the first *lala* he'd met. Proper pronunciation would prevent me from heaping the question with scorn, but I trusted the power of a well-timed smile. I stopped myself, though. I have, over the years, pretended to be so many things. On that night I pretended to be an American who didn't speak Chinese.

I could tell from his expression—like a child sucking hard candy—that Dorian had made the same decision. We listened together as they talked like we weren't there, while Liz grinned and drank her vodka.

"Sam brought you a birthday present, Li Qin. Too bad he had to sacrifice his own date to do it."

"No, he has two dates and neither of them want him!"

"You should've let Li Qin set you up."

"Or even your mother."

"Do they at least let you watch?"

"Leave him alone. Sam likes what he likes," Li Qin said. Then, taking a shot from the bottle of vodka he'd paid for, "And I don't think what he likes is watching women."

Their laughter drowned out everything.

I pushed my straw to the side the way Dorian had done and emptied my drink. Dorian picked up the half-full bottle of vodka Li Qin had just set down, the second he'd paid for at ¥400 apiece. He shrugged his shoulders and walked away with it, taller than the crowd he waded into and still somehow disappearing from view. I followed him, pulling gently on Liz's wrist but then letting it go, wanting only to fade away. If I thought he'd follow us, I would've tugged on Sam's arm, too.

WE STAND WITHOUT MOVING

照片

Though I'm not sure how many more pictures I can stand, I don't stop myself from looking. Liz used to call social media a pointless exercise in self-promotion. No longer pointless, I suppose, now that she had something worth promoting.

The album titles say nothing, but tell me a lot: "Bachelorette Shenanigans," "Let's Plan a Wedding," "Engagement Photo Shoot." Liz's whole life, airbrushed and put on display.

She married Bryan. Their relationship wasn't the mistake; ours was. I wonder what their reunion was like. But for now I stop myself from looking for the pictures because I don't want to know how quickly she got over me.

The first album in her profile is simply called "Shanghai." The cover image is a picture of Liz holding up a Blue Frog martini—I recognize the size of the glass—as though toasting the camera. Her hair is pulled back and she's laughing, her mouth open wider than it is in any of her posed wedding shots. I took the picture, but I can't remember what I said that she'd found so funny.

It's been years since I felt like a tourist in Shanghai, since I carried a camera around with me everywhere, just in case. I wonder if I'll have the urge again when I arrive in Berlin.

Liz took so many pictures that I stopped noticing the camera. Now my mind races, trying to remember what she'd captured.

1.

Love is not a builder and she cannot be built. Almost no one understands this. Love does not have strength or fortitude or courage, but she hopes for these things. She seeks them out. For two weeks I wore Liz's necklace every day. Sam cancelled one coffee with Liz, then a second. The pearls cooled the flush that crept over my chest when I allowed myself to wonder why.

In the mornings that May the smog seemed to dissipate. The sunlight appeared to crack open the sky then, reflecting off the gleaming glass towers; and the older high-rises with their pea green façades glistened like wet bars of soap. The peach blossoms were withered, but still the air carried their scent, like a story almost forgotten. The paper-thin petals wafted to the ground where they were bruised easily, and then ground to nothing.

The crowd at Zapata's was thick, and somewhere in the midst of it was Frank's going away party. Likely other parties, too—it was the season. We recognized people we knew hovering around a table close to the door, and we squeezed in where there was room, deferring a trip to the bar in favor of standing close together with our fingers intertwined. I recalled the freedom I'd felt with Alice, before I understood the way sexuality could be a spectacle. Before I'd gotten scared.

Our expat acquaintances looked at us with eyebrows raised but said nothing as I pushed Liz's hair behind her ear and kissed her bare shoulder lightly, quickly. *Yes,* I wanted to say to them, *yes, it's love you're seeing,* but smiled instead and suggested to Liz that we go find Frank. We left the table to a flurry of whispers that I could almost hear. "Did you just see...?" "So, are they...?" "I guess it makes sense..." The news of our love followed us like an electrified tail, snapping and hopping with a life of its own, through the bar.

We ordered margaritas and joined the crowd. Frank was drunk and wearing a crown on his head just a few feet away. We were approaching the party's center of gravity.

"Sasha!" he shouted as his orbit brought him closer. As though he and I were good friends.

"Hi, Frank! You remember my girlfriend, Liz." She didn't need to be introduced to him anymore than I did, but I said it anyway, enjoying the word girlfriend hovering in the air like an armed dirigible.

"I...do remember Liz. Hi. Thanks for coming."

"So you're headed back for grad school in the fall?" Liz asked.

He sighed loudly and shook his head. "Yeah, it looks that way," as though he wasn't sure how it'd happened.

"That's so exciting!"

"Thanks. Yeah..." Frank's voice trailed off as he put a hand on my shoulder. "I'm headed to the bar. I'll see you later." He stood for a moment longer than was necessary, his hand still pressing upon me, looking at me as though waiting for some final mystery to be revealed.

I willed myself not to think about my father and his

disappointment. He wasn't in that bar and never would be. He can't reach me here.

Liz stared, from Frank to me and back to Frank again. She coughed briefly, as though clearing her throat.

He had not walked far before she began to laugh.

"Did you see his face?" she giggled into her cup. It was a rhetorical question, but I wanted to tell her no. *No. I didn't let myself look at his face.*

Instead I laughed. "He looked like he swallowed a bug." This was fun for Liz, and I was determined to make it fun for me too. I was free.

We continued to circle the bar. Dorian was there somewhere. I wasn't looking but knew I'd find him. He'd gone home with Li Qin's vodka after we left Guandii, "just tired" he'd said and I told myself I believed him.

At Zapata's, Frank found him before we did.

"Dude! Did you know Sasha and Liz were fucking? I can't believe you didn't tell me."

Dorian's sigh was soft. "You're a jackass, Frank."

"What?"

"They're not fucking. Not that it's any of your business."

"Oh, excuse me. I didn't realize they were saving themselves for marriage. Dating, then. Did you know they were dating?"

"They're not fucking dating either. They got drunk and made out once. Which—how do you even know about? And why do you care?"

"I don't care. I just thought you were into her. But when did they make out? You saw them? How did I fucking miss that?"

Dorian needed another drink. A stronger drink. "Why did you say they were fucking if you didn't hear about them making out?" He spoke slowly, as though Frank were a much larger audience Dorian needed to enunciate for.

"They just told me."

For a long time Dorian had been seeing what he wanted to see, as architects do. Even as Frank stood in front of him giggling and imagining Liz and I naked together, Dorian still didn't understand: I wasn't a building he could shade into his sketchbook, or tattoo on his forearm.

He didn't believe Frank, not entirely. Not that he thought Frank was being deliberately misleading, but he was likely very confused. He had to be.

He found me outside the bathroom.

"Frank seems to think you and Liz are lesbians."

I'd come to China to escape the three syllables that would otherwise define my whole life.

I don't care if you're a lesbian, Sasha. But other people you meet in life certainly will. You have to think about the impact of just being open with something like that.

Lesbian. Something like that. There was scorn in my father's voice, masquerading as concern.

I didn't want to live in the closet or pretend to be someone I wasn't. But I'd come to China where I knew no one, so that there would be no one to whom I owed any explanations. But then I got to know people, and they wanted me to account for myself.

"I am," I sighed. "Why do you care? Are you a homophobe?"

"What? No, of course not."

"Great. Then we don't need to talk about it." I just wanted to get back to Liz, who was waiting at the bar.

Dorian touched my wrist as I walked past him, not grabbing or pulling, but holding on to me in a way I found hard to brush off.

"What?" I turned back, and immediately felt that we were standing too close. I observed our proximity, though, like an objective fact that couldn't be changed.

"I didn't imagine it."

"Imagine what?"

"That there's something between us. We have chemistry. I know we do."

"Fine. Yes. We have friendly chemistry. I'm glad that we're friends."

"It's more than that."

He tightened his fingers around my wrist and I wondered what it was like to be so confident. I thought about pulling away, but small acts of decisiveness like that were nearly impossible for me. Leaving the country would have been easier for me than asking Dorian to stop touching me.

Because I stood without moving, because I was looking up at him wondering what I should tell him to avoid causing a scene or hurting his feelings, he kissed me.

"What the fuck?"

I should've been the one to say it, but instead it was Liz.

There were so many things I should've said to him. But I could either yell at Dorian or go after Liz. I chose her. She turned and left, walking as quickly as anyone could without running, parting the crowds in the bar with her hands, with her elbows when necessary, refusing to deviate from her straight path to the exit. She was faster than I was.

When I got outside I saw her getting into a cab. Then she was gone.

That isn't how things ended between us, but maybe it would have been better if they had.

As I stood looking at the space where the car had been, Dorian came up beside me.

"What the fuck is wrong with you?" I screamed.

"I'm sorry! I don't know why I did that. It was way out of line."

"It was sexual assault."

"I didn't assault you, Sasha! That's not what I meant."

He looked to me like a child being scolded for something he'd never explicitly been told not to do, waiting for me to be reasonable, or teach him something. I didn't have the energy.

"Just leave me alone," I said quietly.

"Do you want me to text Liz? I'll tell her it was nothing."

It wasn't nothing, I said in my head. Aloud I just said no.

2.

The next morning, I sat at the dining table, drinking jasmine tea. The dried buds blossomed in the boiling water and then floated there, bobbing against my lip with each sip. I alternated my gaze from the bottom of my cup to the door of the second bedroom, closed since I'd come home last night. I couldn't remember the last time Liz had slept there.

I'd thought about knocking, had several times even approached the door on quiet feet. But I was scared of making things worse. I imagined her packing, booking a flight.

I peed with the bathroom door open, afraid if I didn't that she would leave without saying goodbye. I imagined she was waiting for her chance.

None of the thoughts circling around my head were rational but telling myself that only amplified them. Anxiety is a bully.

Liz and I had been together seven or eight months—I couldn't be sure exactly. I spurned anniversary dates, feeling as I did that they were cursed, though in truth I'd never celebrated one so couldn't say with any certainty. But then we'd been public for only a couple weeks, or maybe just one night, depending on which audience mattered more.

I thought about all those dates, those half-starts and do-overs and wondered what they all meant. Whenever it started, the relationship was the longest I'd ever had up to that point. Which meant, of course, that I expected it to wither and die at any moment. Alternatively, it might have expired months ago, choked on some dumplings and died at our dinner table, while I simply looked on, too stupid to perform the Heimlich. Or, it was just now coming to life.

I finished my tea. Love paced the apartment, Anxiety trailing her like a shadow.

The bedroom door opened and I held my breath. I didn't see any full suitcases over her shoulder, but that didn't mean they weren't there. She wasn't dressed for travel, though, wearing pajama shorts and a t-shirt. My t-shirt. Love exhaled.

Liz looked at me blankly and then went into the bathroom, closing that door behind her, leaving the one to the bedroom ajar. Her silence gave a clue to the kind of fight this would be: she'd sulk, I'd grovel. I rehearsed my lines to the muffled sound of her brushing her teeth.

"Do you want some tea?" I asked when she finally came out. She was standing with her arms crossed outside the bathroom, as though unsure whether she wanted to come into the living room or retreat to her bed.

"No thank you," she answered, her tone formal.

I wished I had thought to go out for a coffee for her.

"Can we talk about last night?"

"I have nothing to say." Petulant. But that was her role. She sat down on the far end of the couch, though, at least willing to be petulant in the same space as me.

"I am so, so sorry. I had no idea Dorian was going to

do that. I was talking to him about you, telling him we were together, and out of nowhere he just kissed me."

"Out of nowhere? Sasha, you've been flirting with him for months. What am I supposed to think?"

"You're supposed to trust me."

"I can't trust you if you don't tell me what the hell's been going on."

"I don't know what to say. Dorian's been my friend for a few years. I don't why he suddenly decided he wanted me. All I wanted was to keep being his friend."

"Are you attracted to him?"

"Liz, I'm gay!"

She looked at me like that hadn't occurred to her before.

Anxiety sat close, making me sweat, until she laughed.

"God, I'm being fucking ridiculous, aren't I?"

"A little bit," I smiled.

"And Jesus, what an entitled asshole he is."

I shrugged. "He's been a good friend for a little while now. Honestly I think the condo thing is just getting to him."

Liz rolled her eyes.

I didn't know how fights were supposed to end. "I really am sorry."

"I know," she said. "It's okay."

I wanted to move to the other end of the couch, her end, to curl my body around hers like a corkscrew. But she stood up before I had the chance. "Let's go to brunch."

The ease of it made me nervous, but I agreed. I wasn't sure I had a choice.

At Element Fresh, the white faces vastly outnumbered the Chinese, unless you counted the waiters. I waved and nodded at many of the people at other tables as Liz and I took our seats.

"It's like you know every expat in Shanghai."

I brought the large menu up in front of my face. "You know them all too. Or the ones who come here anyway." French toast or eggs, I thought, willing myself not to hear accusations in Liz's voice. French toast or eggs.

"I don't know any of them."

"What are you talking about? You know everyone I do." I began naming the people I'd waved to, reminding Liz of the happy hour where we'd last run into each other, the conversations we'd had.

Our waiter came over, interrupting my list of all the friends Liz supposedly had to take our order, forcing me to make a decision. Liz ordered an omelet and a mimosa. I chose the French toast.

"No mimosa?" she asked me before the waiter put away his pen.

"I wasn't going to drink."

"What's the point of brunch, then?" She laughed but I thought I heard an edge. I missed the menu; my fingertips clutched at the white table top. Everything in the restaurant seemed smooth and white and healthy and slippery, an antidote to the grime and humidity of the streets outside. I felt like I might slide off my plastic chair into a puddle beneath our table.

I nodded my head at the waiter and he added a second mimosa to our order. When he came back with them, I sat looking at the champagne flute, wishing instead for the solidity of a Bloody Mary: a glass I could wrap my entire hand around, a straw to slurp through, a vegetable garden of garnishes bobbing on tiny spears—something I could organize on my bread plate, something I could control.

"Are you meeting Sam today?" I forced myself to attempt normal conversation. Things were fine. It was only my head that was spinning.

"Oh. I haven't heard from him." She sounded like it was only now occurring to her. "That's kind of weird." She took out her phone, ready to text him.

"Do you think he's upset?"

"What would he be upset about?"

"The birthday party. We were…I mean…we probably took him by surprise, don't you think?" I'd never told her what I overheard his friends saying that night before we left.

She shrugged. "He already knew we were dating. I'm sure it's fine. I'll see if he wants to have coffee sometime this week."

I could've told her.

She sent the text and put her phone back in her bag. We finished our drinks and ordered two more. Our food arrived and then my mouth was too full of food, my head still too full of worry, to say anything. We were fine and Dorian was fine and Sam was fine. Liz's job was fine. Things were only wrong in my head.

3.

We stepped off the school bus on Monday morning, with the sun shining and the air surprisingly crisp, feeling more like the beginning of the school year than the end. We had only a few more weeks to go.

"Did you keep the lesson plans I handed in last week?" I asked Liz quietly as we stood in the crowded hallway outside the main office.

"Yes, of course." Since the disastrous observation, Liz had been doing her best to follow the plans I gave her. She complained about the job more frequently, but I took that to mean she was working harder, and that her teaching was therefore better.

"Okay, good. I'll see you at lunch." I touched her hand, gently squeezing her pinkie between my thumb and forefinger. And that was it. I ducked into the office and Liz went upstairs to the computer lab, where she wasted the 45 minutes before her first class.

She arrived a few minutes early for Ms. Rose's class and slowed her approach as she saw Madeline standing outside the door. She needs to speak with Ms. Rose, Liz thought. She'll catch her on the way out of the class and the two women will disappear down the hall, never looking back.

Madeline nodded to her as she neared the door but said nothing and Liz felt a wave of relief that she'd been correct. But then Ms. Rose came out of the room and Madeline only nodded again, and then held the door open for Liz, motioning her to enter first, clearly indicating that she would follow. Liz had no choice but to go in.

She stopped at the back of the class, turning toward Madeline, still hoping there was perhaps something simple that her boss needed to tell her before she would leave.

"Whenever you're ready, dear. I'll just be right back here."

"Yes, of course."

She clutched the lesson plan as she walked to the front of her room, knowing at least that it matched the one on Madeline's clipboard. It didn't matter. Liz's classes that morning—three of them in a row—went exactly as they usually did: her students spoke without raising their hands, got up out of their seats without asking permission; they watched her write the focusing question on the board and then, after she read it aloud to them, they all began talking at once in response. Nothing that I wrote on a lesson plan could tell Liz how to manage 25 seven-year-olds. She'd mostly stopped noticing the chaos, telling herself it was just the nature of an unstructured class like speech. They were talking, after all. The look on Madeline's face after the first class ended, though, suggested she disagreed.

Two hours later, Liz tried to remain calm as she hurried through the crowds of students in the cafeteria. I was already sitting at our usual table.

Liz sat down and spoke quietly. "Why did you ask me if I had my lesson plans?"

"What do you mean?"

I'm sure I sounded to Liz like I was playing dumb. "You asked if I had my lesson plans. Why? You never ask me that."

"How did it go?"

"How did you know she was coming?" Liz countered.

I bit on a hangnail, then picked at something under my fingernail. "I set it up," I answered, finally looking up at her.

She took a deep breath. I heard the clatter of silverware against the dishes, the shrieking of students at the surrounding tables. They were all excited for the end of the school year. Everyone wanted to get out.

"Why would you do that?"

"I had to, Liz. I'm trying to save your job! They're making staffing decisions for next year and I heard Madeline telling Principal Wu that she didn't know if you used your lesson plans. I asked her to give you a second chance, as a favor." I spoke quickly now, as though afraid Liz might walk away before I was finished. I hadn't expected her to be angry with me.

"Why didn't you tell me?"

"Madeline told me she'd do another observation, but only if it was a surprise. She didn't think it would be fair for you to have another chance you knew about, since none of the other teachers do. I couldn't tell you."

"You could've told me and trusted me to not to let on! You could've helped me prepare."

"I'm helping you as much as I can, Liz."

I'd been expecting gushing gratitude, didn't know what to do with the anger I was getting instead.

"No one made you hire me, you know." She looked deflated.

No one made you apply, I wanted to say, but thought better of it.

"I'm sorry I didn't warn you. I really was just trying to help."

"I know. It's okay."

"So how did it go?"

"It was fantastic," she told me. "I did great."

I still don't know whether she believed that herself or not.

4.

Shanghai makes promises: it will rocket the world's fastest train levitating through a magnetic tube; will erect buildings that look like space shuttles, that make you believe you can fly; will increase production and earnings and the reach of its tentacled highways out into the surrounding country. Shanghai promises, promises and then forgets, moves on to the next. Shanghai will leave you behind.

But not Dorian. He stared down at the piece of paper he'd received in the mail from the Office of Foreign Investment. It didn't say very much, but still he had read it at least 10 times since opening it. The only thing to do was to call his real estate agent. He was stalling, though—washing his dishes, straightening the books on his coffee table, making his bed. When there was nothing left to do in his apartment, when he found himself simply walking in circles, touching some object or another on each rotation, he finally picked up his cell phone. He wondered as he dialed whether she would even remember him—it had been so long since their last meeting—and he thought briefly about hanging up, but then he heard her voice on the other end of the line.

He said his name, adding "the American" in case she did in fact need a reminder as to who he was, though it was doubtful this identifier alone would help.

She seemed to recognize him, or else was good at pretending she did. "Yes, hello," she said in Chinese.

"I have my foreign investor," he said, looking down at the paper as he did, as though the information might have changed since the last time he read it.

He wasn't sure what kind of reaction he was expecting: a whoop and a shout perhaps, a congratulations, though of course he'd done nothing but wait months and months for the news. He heard no emotion in her voice, however. "Very good," she said. "When can you come in?"

They set up an appointment for later that day—no time like the present—after Dorian confirmed that it was not necessary (nor even possible) to contact his investor. The man's name would simply be added to Dorian's application, along with the official seal from the investment office. He would own a small stake in Dorian's new condo, as though those freshly painted walls, the tile and hardwood floors, the granite countertops that Dorian envisioned in his mind were a company that had just gone public. Dorian would pay the man a monthly fee, through the Office of Foreign Investment, a dividend for owning stock in his life.

Still staring at the paper, he forgot for the moment that this man—Deng Yongrui—had been randomly assigned to him by a bureaucrat in some poorly lit, smoke-filled office. He imagined instead that Deng Yongrui had sought him out, had chosen Dorian's apartment, Dorian's life, to buy into. Dorian was, Deng Yongrui believed, a safe investment. He took some confidence from this and shook off the months of doubt that had been clinging to him like a thin layer of dust. He would buy an apartment, for himself and for Deng Yongrui.

The same week that Dorian got his apartment, Liz finally made a plan that Sam didn't cancel. It was obvious to me that he was avoiding her, but she refused to think anything of it, made excuses about his workload or his mother, surely the same excuses Sam peddled to her every time he texted to say he couldn't make it after all. Too polite to either ignore or confront her, he was simply hoping she would go away.

I knew what would happen when she finally forced Sam to see her. His lines ran in my head like a script. I could've recited them to her before she left, but I imagined too many scenarios in which she heard jealousy in my caution. So I said nothing.

She beat him to the Starbucks and contemplated buying him a Mocha Frappuccino. He hadn't done that for her again after that first meeting, but she was sure he'd remember. She didn't have time to execute, realizing for the first time how early Sam must've been that afternoon to have had her drink on the table when she arrived. After 10 minutes of waiting that morning, Liz was still four patrons away from the register when Sam stepped in line just beside her. She ordered an iced latte, and unable to surprise him with a drink, asked him what he'd like.

He shook his head. "Nothing. I'm okay."

When she asked him where he wanted to sit, he shrugged.

Remembering what he'd said once about helping her find a better job if she ever needed one, she was eager to talk to him about her second observation. It hadn't gone terribly—or at least it could have been worse—but she wanted to know what her options might be. She hated the job, so even if she did get asked back, maybe she'd want to do something else. Wrapped up as she was in her own issues, she barely noticed Sam's detachment.

"I'm so glad we finally found a time to get together. You've been so busy!"

He looked down at the table Liz had chosen. "I haven't been busy," he admitted. "I was waiting for you to apologize."

"Apologize? For what?"

"For what you did at Li Qin's birthday party."

Even then Liz didn't understand. She blinked. "I'm sorry. I know we left in a hurry. I think Dorian felt sick or something. I don't know. They just ran out of there. But I should've said good night."

"Saying good night would've made things even worse."

"Sam, what are you talking about?"

"You were supposed to be my date." He looked up at her for the first time, then. "You embarrassed me. You and Sasha."

"I—I'm…" She sighed. "I don't know what to say."

Sam glared at her. The thing to say was obvious.

She got there, but the awkward silence that came first made everything worse. "I'm really sorry. I didn't know Sasha was going to come to the party. I told her not to, actually! But honestly, I think she was jealous. Or worried something was going to happen, which is ridiculous. I told her it was a pretend date, but I don't know. I don't know what she was thinking. I really didn't have any idea she was going to come."

Her explanation came out in a rush, none of it any interest to Sam. It was all he was going to get from her though. Life happened to Liz: Bryan had happened and the job in Shanghai had happened and then I had happened, over and over again I happened. Sam happened to her, too, but he was a secondary character: what she did to him was of no concern.

"And I'm sorry I have failed you as a language partner."
He stood up. Liz still had three-quarters of an iced latte in
a glass tumbler to finish. She didn't know where Sam was
going.

"What do you mean? You haven't failed."

"You haven't learned any Chinese."

"I know, but…the sessions are still really helpful." She
felt like a child looking up at him from her seat at the table.
If she stood she would've been able to make eye contact
with him, but she wasn't sure she wanted that.

"I'm not so worried about learning Chinese," she
continued. "I just thought we were friends."

"You're not a very good friend," he answered. And that
was it. He turned and left the Starbucks, shoving his hands
in his pockets as he walked away.

Liz blinked her eyes and watched him go. She finished
her latte, though it tasted metallic to her now, bitter. First,
she blamed me. She'd told me not to come and I hadn't
listened. She'd told me she wanted to be a good friend to
Sam and I had sabotaged her.

As she fumed, though, she also remembered—the
way it felt when I'd kissed her in front of everyone, the
greed with which she'd soaked up my attention, the ease
with which she'd forgotten all about Sam and the favor
she'd promised him. She remembered, too, the warning
I'd given over brunch, when I'd gently suggested that Sam
might have been upset. The anger toward me she balanced
against her own shame; she could fight with me, sure, but
then she'd have to admit that Sam was right: she hadn't
been a good friend to him.

I wish she trusted me enough to share that shame.
If I could change anything that happened between us, it
would've been this: *I know how he looked at you*, I would
have told her.

She said nothing to me, though, collecting secrets like
beads on a necklace.

5.

Love mourned the loss of stars. She'd danced giddily in the neon for too many nights. She dreamt of beaches in the moonlight, yes, with the rain clouds swelling. She wanted romance and muffled sweaty sex beneath the blankets at the hostel and cold gritty sex on the mostly deserted beach, and to escape the sooty humidity of Shanghai which made Love feel grimy and old.

Love made some convincing arguments. A vacation would have done Liz and me some good, but I couldn't muster the energy to plan anything. The spring had taken its emotional toll; recalling the cozy winter Liz and I had spent burrowed into our apartment, I was feeling the urge to nest. Liz, like Love, was looking for an escape.

It might have turned into a fight, but as the school year neared its end, we weren't having the kinds of conversations that led anywhere, either good or bad. Four martinis into a night at Blue Frog—where no real conversation between two people has ever occurred—I decided to give it a try.

"Are you okay? You've seemed kind of unhappy lately."

Liz shrugged. "What does happiness even look like?" she mumbled, expecting the question to slip unnoticed into the air between us, drowned out by the bar's early '90s juke box.

I heard her, though. I was listening.

"You really don't know, do you?"

Liz turned away from me and drained her martini. "When I was in the fourth grade, we had to write these books: 'Happiness Is…' they were called. Each page we wrote something that made us happy. Mine was the longest." As though that proved something indelible about her character.

"What did you write about?"

"I can't remember."

"Well, there you have it." I looked down at the shoes that brought me eye level with her, or would have, were we making any eye contact. I thought briefly about driving my right high-heel down into my own left toe. But what would that solve?

Blue Frog was narrow, with a long black bar stretching across one end of the place and a row of tall black tables against the opposite wall. There were never enough barstools. I leaned with my elbows propped on the table behind us, scanning the room rather than looking at Liz.

"Have you thought at all about what we should do this summer?"

She shrugged, again, as I knew she would. The open-ended question was a ruse, an opening to a monologue I'd already planned.

"I was thinking maybe we could look for a new apartment." I said it slowly, into my empty martini glass.

"What's wrong with the apartment?"

Our apartment, I wanted to correct her. But that was part of the problem; it had remained mine.

"Nothing, I guess. But I've been there a few years, and

a change would be nice. I want a place that feels like ours, that we can furnish on our own, with things we choose. Together."

Blue Frog's oversized martinis were slightly ridiculous, like something the Flintstones would drink when they were feeling fancy. They made me brave. Our table was in the corner, close to the door. Love counted the steps, had not ruled out the possibility that she would have to make a quick exit.

"What if I lose my job?"

"What are you talking about?"

"It's possible, Sasha. They might not ask me back. What would I do if I signed a new lease and then had to move home?"

Home, I heard. *I*. I wanted to correct her: *What would we do if you had to find a new job*. She was flubbing her lines.

"I need another drink," I said instead.

"Definitely."

We made our way up to the bar, then back to our corner table, the two of us safe again behind freshly chilled glasses.

"Is this what you want?"

Liz nodded. "It's really good. Do you want a sip?" She held her pink cocktail out to me.

"Not the drink, Liz," I snapped. "This. Us. Are you done with us? Was it a fun experiment for you? Did you just need a guide to show you around Shanghai?"

Liz must have understood that I was looking for only one answer, though I realize now the three questions were very different. She didn't parse. "No. No, I'm not done."

"Okay," I said. I believed her, I think. But Love sighed and rolled her eyes. She wandered out into the night.

"It will be fun to decorate a new place," I said after we were silent for a few minutes, settling in to the promise I'd chosen to hear.

"It will," she agreed.

I finished my martini and set the glass down on the table behind us with purpose, as though I were planning to begin immediately looking for a new place to live. Liz followed me out the door.

6.

Expats throw parties. It's part of the point of being in Shanghai. The new ones—recently out of college, intoxicated by the idea of seeing relative strangers half-naked—favor theme parties: anything but clothes, '50s pajamas. After a year or two most of them learn that the beer still works no matter what they're wearing, and that jeans and a tank top are easier to shed than a crepe paper costume designed to look like a bouquet of flowers. Easier to put back on, too.

Expats throw parties in the apartments furnished by our Chinese landlords. We offer tours of whatever oddities our homes happen to contain: the stand-up steam shower or the convection oven or the door into the bedroom that is only four feet high. We stock our bars with Great Wall red wine and Tsingtao and ask our friends to smoke only in the hallway outside the apartment, or in the elevator, like all the neighbors do.

We didn't often throw surprise parties, though; we didn't often know anyone well enough to bother surprising.

But I was planning one for Liz.

It wasn't an entirely generous notion.

I wanted to celebrate—we'd made it through the school year, were planning to look at new apartments—but I wasn't sure Liz, in her recent sour mood, would've let me.

So I planned it without telling her and called it a surprise.

I sent the invitation the same way they always went out: to the group text saved in my phone, on everyone's phones. More than half the numbers I didn't recognize, but if they were on the group text they got the invite. I didn't have to make sure to take Liz out of the group because I had never put her in. She still didn't understand how we all always knew which bar to end up at.

Expats threw parties, and yet Dorian had gone eight months without attending one, two years at least without hosting his own. That was back when he had roommates: Jeff and what's-his-name, the quiet one who always got too drunk too quickly and passed out, ending up with Sharpie on his face more times than anyone could remember. Karl! Jeff and Karl. Their apartment was the dream of a rich guy frat house for people who, back in the States, weren't rich and wouldn't have been let in to any frats. Dorian stayed for a little over a year before he found his own place.

At the time, it had seemed like a step backward. He didn't throw parties, didn't even want to invite friends over, picturing them spinning in circles in the small lobby of his building, desperate to believe that somewhere—maybe behind the plastic plant in the corner, or through the random broom closet—there was an elevator that would carry them up to the seventh floor. You have to walk up, and oh, there are no lights in the stairwell: these were words that Dorian couldn't imagine saying to any of his friends. Which perhaps suggested he didn't really have any friends after all.

Drunk women, the ones with uptight roommates, or the ones so new to Shanghai that they were still crashing on someone's couch, had seen his apartment, but they didn't spend much time looking around. In the morning they were hung over and either embarrassed or regretful or freaking out about some boyfriend somewhere; they didn't linger.

Which is to say, Dorian was in the mood to go to a party, and certainly wouldn't be throwing one himself.

He'd closed on a new condo; he had something worth celebrating. The invitation I hadn't intended to send him came at just the right time.

The last day of school finally arrived. Together Liz and I watched the chaos of children taking leave.

"You made it," I said to her. We were leaning against my desk, looking out into the hallway. It was still the middle of the day, but students had been given time to clear their lockers; the teachers were mainly in the staff room, organizing their desks. Students finished their work quickly and then ran up and down the halls, in and out of classrooms.

Soon they would file out the door into the suffocating humidity, kicking up the dust from the driveway as they went, shouting their goodbyes to each other. Mostly they went back to their home countries for the summer, which made the goodbyes more difficult, though they all seemed excited to be reunited with long-lost neighborhood friends. The school year was a lifetime for them, the summertime yet another. They could unfold and unfold, born all over again every week if they wanted. I remembered what it was like.

"Just barely," Liz answered.

I laughed, though I knew she wasn't kidding.

"I should clean my desk."

"Stay." I'd never had someone to watch the melee with. "Leave it for next year. It'll give you something to do your first day back."

Liz shifted her weight. "Oh, God, I don't want to have to deal with it then. Come with me. It won't take long. I'm just going to throw everything away."

Convinced the teachers saw me as a spy, I didn't go often to the staffroom. They'd stop their conversations, suddenly searching through a drawer or opening up a textbook whenever I passed, as though I might have been instructed to compile reports about how they spent their free time. As though anyone cared.

The last day would be different, though. There were teachers at almost every desk, most of them sitting with stacks of paper in their laps and trash cans at their feet.

"Keep the lesson plans," I hissed, trying to keep my voice down as I saw Liz reach for a trash can. "Keep the ones I made for you. You'll need those."

She shrugged and headed toward her desk. I didn't understand what that meant. There were no free chairs, so I paced the perimeter of the room, trying not to look at anyone in particular, hoping not to appear nosy about what they were throwing away.

I passed the staff mailboxes and looked in, just glancing with no purpose, though I realized it looked even more like I was snooping. I stopped and looked around; no one was watching me anyway. No one cared.

Liz's mailbox was full, certainly containing more than one day's worth of mail. I sighed, wondering how often she bothered to check. Next year would be different, I told myself. Liz would have a year of experience, would understand the school and its politics and would have the lesson plans all ready to go.

I reached for the mail, noticing as I did that the memos on the bottom of the stack were at least a week old. I furrowed my brow, wondering if there was any point in talking to her about it. She needed to understand that the people who filled the mailboxes noticed such things, but then, what good would it do that day? I should've checked on this long before.

Likely there was nothing important in the stack of memos, but I wanted to know for sure.

"Are you stealing my mail?"

I jumped. "No, of course not." I thrust the pile of unread paper to her, hoping she intended to look through them rather than throwing them away.

"Thanks." Liz smiled and shoved the pile into her bag. "Want to head back downstairs? This place is depressing. At least the kids are happy about the end of school."

I looked around, noticing for the first time the dour expressions on all the teachers' faces. It was nothing new; they always looked that way.

"Sure." I followed Liz out of the room, down the hallway, and then the stairs back to the office. I wanted to ask how she knew she still had a job next year if she hadn't looked through her mail in a week, but then had the superstitious feeling that asking the question could somehow cause her firing. If the school needed to hire a new speech teacher, I told myself, I'd know about it already.

The day wore on and it was easy to distract myself. Students stopped into the office periodically to say goodbye. Mostly they were third, fourth, and fifth graders who visited me over the school year—the sensitive, homesick ones, old enough to know they couldn't cry in their classrooms. They asked for passes to the bathroom and would come to my office instead. I'd give them water and let them sit on the couch for a moment, let them draw a picture or write in a journal or do whatever they needed to do. A few of them had cards for me. I smiled and gave them hugs, though touching the students was discouraged. Then they ran off.

At the end of the day we watched the students file out of the building and then went to our last staff meeting of the year. An hour and a half later, we were creeping through Shanghai's early evening traffic. Our goodbyes all said, we were ready for something new.

7.

I wanted to ask Liz if she was going to look through her mail. The bag sat at her feet during the entire ride home. Traffic lurched, but the bag with the mail didn't move. *We could look at it together,* I might have suggested. *I could look at it for you.* It wasn't the worry that I was being invasive that kept me quiet. I would've sorted through the pile without telling her if I had the chance. But I didn't want to speak my anxieties. Saying things aloud makes them true.

As we neared our intersection my worries found new perches on which to alight: the party waiting in our apartment, the celebration I hoped Liz would want. She liked attention, I knew; I hoped that translated into liking surprises.

It was impossible not to hear the noise from our apartment as we walked down the hall. Liz looked at me without turning her head and I pretended not to notice.

"What's going on?" she asked as I unlocked the door that wasn't locked. I said nothing.

No one was hiding. It wasn't that kind of party. No

one jumped out and yelled, "Surprise!" The people nearest to the door turned when we entered and said hello. Liz looked at me instead of at them.

"Surprise," I said quietly. She looked nervous rather than happy.

"Is this for me?"

I nodded, but it didn't seem to be the answer she wanted. "For us," I corrected. "End of the school year, goodbye to the apartment. All that."

"We haven't even found a new place."

We were still standing just inside the door. I edged us toward the kitchen where there was vodka and cranberry juice to make it pink. "It's a party," I told her, as though the what could replace the why. "Parties are fun." I waved vaguely at the people in the other room, hoping their presence proved something.

"I guess I should change," she said, taking the cocktail I'd made for her out of my hand, draining half of it in one sip before leaving the kitchen.

I laughed and offered her a refill before she went, knowing Drunk Liz would be more fun. She brought her bag, overstuffed with papers from work, with her.

I put the mail out of mind and sipped my drink. *Parties are fun*, I thought.

I don't know whether Dorian arrived before Liz and me, or if he came in while Liz was changing. But there he was in the kitchen, opening my refrigerator to help himself to a beer.

I should've realized he got the invitation, but it hadn't occurred to me to worry about it because it never occurred to me he would come.

"Wow." It was all I could think to say.

"Hey! You're here."

"I live here."

"I know that. But you weren't here before."

"Okay, yes. I'm here. We're both here, apparently."

"I bought a condo." He sucked the foam off the top of his can, looking pleased with himself.

"That's great." I wanted to get past him, but he was blocking the door. I could have excused myself or asked him to get out of my way but I just stood there, waiting for him to notice the space he occupied.

He didn't move, instead started telling me about his condo. I didn't care about his balcony or his recessed lighting. I made myself another drink while he talked, not even bothering to nod politely because he wouldn't have noticed if I had. He was talking about the bidding process when someone who cared about Dorian's new life came in for a beer. I took the opportunity to escape.

Liz was sitting on the couch, somehow managing to make a sparkly tank top look sullen. Everyone around her was standing. I made a mental note that she didn't like surprises. She needed another drink. Over my shoulder in the kitchen I heard Dorian mention his interest rate. *She can have my drink*, I thought, and I crossed the apartment to give it to her.

"Dorian's here." There was no point trying to hide it from her.

"Why would you invite him?" She spoke loudly, emphasizing each word more than the last. I expected her to ask why he would come, which is not such a different question, except that the one she asked I couldn't answer by shrugging and calling him an asshole.

"I didn't really mean to."

She folded her arms across her chest and glared at me. "How do you *accidentally* invite someone to a party?" She was practically snarling.

"Is it really that big a deal? We don't have to talk to him."

"Oh, no. I can't wait to talk to him. I'm going to spend all night talking to him."

"You seem a lot more upset than is necessary." Just

because it was true didn't make it the right thing to say.

She stood abruptly, leaving me sitting alone on the couch.

"I need a drink." Handing me back the glass I'd brought for her, now empty, she stomped toward the kitchen like a child.

I wasn't trying to be condescending or obtuse. I was genuinely confused by the sudden change in her mood. But I couldn't make her talk to me.

Love liked a good party. She didn't drink, but she enjoyed the false confidence that rose out of wine glasses like steam. It wasn't really bravery, only Love knew, that propelled one person across a room toward another. It was fear.

Liz emerged from the kitchen with her drink—pale pink and with not enough ice to even make it palatable. I wanted to shake her a proper cocktail; providing a lesson on the comforts offered by tiny ice crystals floating in your drink would have made me feel like my father. The thought made me smile, which told me I had been drinking just the right amount myself: enough to soften the edges of my memories until they appeared blurry and romantic, not so much that they became stabbingly sharp.

I grew up watching my step-mother host. She fluttered like a hummingbird, alighting from one cluster of people to the next, pleasing everyone. I watched her parties like they were a soap opera in which nothing bad ever happened: it was just rich people making Manhattans. Everyone laughing at the same time.

That night I didn't have the energy to play the role of hostess; I was back to my place against the wall, watching Liz. Her mood left invisible trails that I felt filling the apartment like smoke. She was doing a remarkable job keeping her distance from me, as though she and I were foosball players tethered to the same pole.

She had joined a small group of people surrounding

Dorian, all of them laughing at the tale of the bureau-cratic horrors he'd successfully navigated. I'd heard the story—each telling from a distance—three times already; he was sharpening it, I could tell, adjusting the timing of his punch lines, embellishing the difficulties he'd had to endure. He'd done nothing, really. Nothing but wait, and even that couldn't be counted as patience since I knew he did it not out of virtue but because he lacked the creativity to choose any other course of action.

Liz was laughing, though I knew she'd heard it already too. As I watched her toast Dorian with another subpar drink, I felt gripped by the need to tell my own story of triumph. Liz was not a new apartment, and there'd been no Chinese bureaucrat standing between us, but still I felt as though I'd won something. No: Dorian had won some-thing, standing around as he had, waiting for a letter in the mail; I had made something, had created love and inter-dependency out of red wine and orgasms, half-truths and Chinese culture lessons, poetic license and a storyteller's sense of delusion and grandeur. Where was my toast?

Love didn't have an answer.

I might've learned from Dorian: it was all in the telling. After his third or fourth recitation, the fourth or fifth drink, Dorian started to sound like he expected the accolades, as though the party had been thrown in his honor. Sure, he'd merely followed the instructions laid out for him by his real estate agent; he'd filled out the right forms, showed up at the right buildings, stood in the interminable lines. Anyone could have done it. But so few people did.

"Most people would've just given up. Or really, I bet most people wouldn't even attempt it in the first place," Liz said.

"I really feel like it's a mistake to see our lives here as

temporary, simply because we're strangers in a strange land. If we were in the states, no one would think twice about me buying a condo."

"Well, maybe not. But 30 still seems pretty young to be able to do that."

Dorian shrugged. "So I'm remarkable for putting my money in a savings account instead of spending it all on beer. That would hardly warrant congratulations back home."

Liz nodded.

"What's remarkable here is not that I'm able to do this. Look around this party." He waved his hand in a sweeping gesture encompassing the living room and all the people in it. "I would bet that half the people in here have the money to do what I'm doing. And really, what I did was not so different than what you'd do in the States. Back home, you get your money together, you get mortgage preapproval, you go house hunting, you put down an offer on something, you hope the sale goes through. Here, you get your money together, you get your foreign investor, you put your bid down on something, and you hope it goes through. Exactly the same."

"So we should all stop congratulating you then," said Liz.

"No, but you should know what you're congratulating. All these people—" again the sweeping arm, "—they're in awe because I'm daring to declare permanence. I'm not just buying a condo; it's a way for me to say that yes, I've chosen to stay in China. No, it's not an experiment, and it's not me refusing to grow up. It's not me hiding from the real world. I'm not killing time here, building my résumé, or waiting for my company to move me somewhere else, like some piece in their multinational board game. All these people toast me because they can't imagine making any kind of permanent decision about anything."

Dorian took a long sip from his beer, that pause

allowing him to hear what an asshole he sounded like.

"Now, hopefully you were recording all of that, and will be able to play it back for my mother when she calls."

"Is she going to care?"

Dorian glared, as though she'd just asked if his mother loved him.

"That's not what I mean. I mean, is she going to be upset that you're staying?"

"I assume so? But then, who knows. Maybe she thinks it's glamorous. My older brother lives in fucking Tucson. You can't get worse than that."

Liz nodded again.

"The new place has a guest room," Dorian continued, "And I'm hoping to get her to come visit. I think she'd like it here." Dorian had missed his chance for the family Christmas he'd hoped for, by almost half a year, but still he looked forward to a visit.

If they went to the markets he'd haggle for her, though she wouldn't really want the knock-off sneakers or purse or whatever it was that caught her attention. If they saw a woman holding her baby out in front of her he'd usher his mother away before it peed on her shoes. At the crosswalks he'd steer her away from the mopeds and bikes, and on the sidewalks away from the raw fish water, the scum-coated puddles. She'd probably hate all of it, but she'd pretend to enjoy it, or at least talk about how much she was learning. She'd be suspicious of the food and appalled by people's pushiness, by the noise and the traffic and the smog that was all so different from Portland. These were all part of the appeal of Shanghai to him: it might as well have been called Not-Portland. He knew, too, that while his mother wouldn't enjoy the visit, she'd see the ways in which Dorian fit here—all the ways he'd never fit in back home—and it would make her happy.

"How about your parents?" Dorian asked. "Are they eager for you to come home?"

"I guess," she answered. "Honestly I haven't thought much about it. I think they know that even if I come back, I'm not going to move back *home* home. I think they see Shanghai as a pretty interesting place for me to live. At least, I hope they do."

"You mean when."

"Sorry?"

"You said if. *If* I come home. You mean when."

"How do you know I mean when? What makes you think I won't stay?"

Dorian cocked his head, studying Liz. "I just know," he said.

Liz laughed, though Dorian hadn't been joking. "I don't really see Sasha going back to the States anytime soon."

"I agree."

She stared at him, as he first rolled up the sleeves of his plaid cotton shirt, and then brushed his straight brown hair out of his eyes. He needed a haircut, and new pants. The jeans he wore now sagged a bit and he was always tugging them back up.

"God, are you always such an asshole?"

"What?"

"You essentially just told me that my relationship was doomed to fail. You realize that, right?"

"What, you thought you were going to marry her or something?" He laughed.

"If she were a guy, or if I were, would you be asking that?"

"If she were a guy, she'd be the guy you were currently sleeping with. So, yeah, I would."

"You don't know us. And you don't really know me."

Dorian put up his hands, surrendering. "Okay, okay. She's your one true love and you guys are going to live together forever, in China. You just don't talk to each other at parties and always seem to be fighting about something."

I used to imagine that she slapped him: loudly enough to silence the room, to turn all heads in their direction; that she let everyone imagine the worst they could about him while he stood there stunned, cheek flaming.

Now I think it's more likely that she laughed: a chuckle at first, and then her head tossed back, mouth wide. White teeth gleaming like pearls.

I was in our bedroom at the time and so I don't really know. I was looking at the remnants of Liz's hasty attempt to get ready: two rejected shirts, a hairbrush fuzzy with use. Her purse was on the floor leaning against the leg of the bed, still overstuffed with the mail she'd brought home from school. I pulled out the stack, casually, as though it were mine. Much of it was junk, but in the middle of the pile was a paper that was thicker than the rest. I recognized Principal Wu's signature on the bottom, the school's logo on the top. In between: "The administration will not be renewing your contract next year."

My first instinct was to shred the paper, as though by destroying the letter I could erase its intent. But I knew ripping it up would change nothing. After destruction I tended toward secrecy. Tucking the paper into the keepsake box in my closet would no more get Liz's job back than destroying it would, but I opened the wooden lid anyway. Atop my passport near the bottom of the box I found the e-mail Liz had sent when she applied for the job, the cover letter I'd rewritten for her, wanting as soon as I read it for the job to be hers. She'd been besotted before she ever arrived, and so was I.

Eventually the party ended. After tucking Liz—too drunk to remember she was angry—into bed, I cleaned up the mess of beer bottles and sticky cocktail glasses, the goblets stained with lipstick and containing the remnants of sweet

Chinese wine. I couldn't sleep.

Three-thirty in the morning is a neon twilight in Shanghai. There was no sun yet, and most of the bars and restaurants still had their signs lit, though few of them were open.

Three-thirty in the morning is the best time to walk around Shanghai. Breezes blow, cool at that time of year, though the asphalt is still hot to the touch. Cars still honk, tires squeal, somewhere a bus groans and firecrackers pop, but at 3:30 they register as individual noises, each shouting in its own voice up into the starless grey sky. And on the residential side streets, the city actually seems dark, and quiet for brief moments, and it's possible to remember that you are alone. Maybe I already knew what was coming.

I ended up at a crowded all-night dumpling house, finding something wonderful in the harsh fluorescent light inside, the crowds of people—all Chinese—waiting in line for their dumplings, the flat-bottomed paper bowls, like boats floating atop the red plastic trays, the sauce bar with its ramekins and tiny ladles. I bought dumplings that I didn't want to eat so I could sit in that space for just a little while.

When I got home, Liz was still asleep. I undressed quietly in the dark, removing the pearl necklace last. Without pausing, I put it inside the wooden box, alongside everything else I was hiding from Liz.

SAYING THINGS ALOUD
MAKES THEM TRUE

Memory shapeshifts. That's not a trick or a malfunction, but its very purpose: We make sense of things by rearranging them. And at the same time we take the photographs we imagine will hold things in place.

Liz's Shanghai is barely recognizable to me, the show she stages one I've never seen.

We are in a crowd of people in front of Guandii, the group of us a mass of open-mouthed smiles and arms draped casually over shoulders. Our heads are tipped back to the sky.

We walk arm in arm toward the photographer, Liz and I in the center of a line of people. Whoever held Liz's camera must have been walking backward, away from us. We turn our heads inward toward each other, ignoring him.

Eight of us cram on a couch in someone's too-small living room, sitting on top of each other to all fit in the frame. We hold our beer bottles carefully so as not to obscure anyone else's face.

There's an artful one of five shots of Jäger lined up on the bar. The second one is empty.

There are students posing with Liz in selfies, all of them giving the peace sign.

Liz's students standing in two rows she arranged in front of the whiteboard. It was the last day of school and they vibrated with joy.

There's a line of yellow school busses.

Liz and I stand beside each other in my office, smiling like co-workers, my shoulder touching her arm. The picture is blurry, taken by a second-grader who needed cheering up.

Sam takes a picture of Liz smiling with a Starbucks mug—a ceramic one, the kind they only give you in China—next to her cheek. Then he hands her the camera and takes up his own mug, mirroring her pose for the picture to set beside hers.

Liz takes a picture of a tea presentation. Liz takes a picture of her soup dumplings. Liz takes a picture of a Teppanyaki chef, his mouth open in controlled astonishment as he looks up at the shrimp flying into his hat. In the foreground of the shot I can make out our drinks: cold beer, hot sake, sweet plum wine. Teppanyaki is all you can drink. We had no reason to choose.

There are Dorian and Frank at Zapata's. There are Liz and Dorian at Blue Frog.

We are dancing at Park 97, our faces practically neon in the camera flash reflected in the strobes.

We are asleep on a tour bus.

I am in the thick of a crowd at Xiangyang Market, a row of white tents in the background just over my head. The picture is too quiet to really be Shanghai.

Liz takes pictures of me; I take pictures of Liz.

We take a picture of the sculpture. She is free, leaping into the air with nothing but the wind to catch her, and she is tethered to the ground.

On the days when Liz fell asleep with her head against the bus window, I nudged her awake as we approached.

"Here she comes," I'd whisper and Liz would straighten, fasten her gaze. If I was the one sleeping, she'd do the same for me. We hated when we missed her.

The picture I want to see is of the two of us the day we found her: I'm kissing Liz's cheek while she stretches her arm out and points the camera back at us. Her smile is broad and she looks at the lens head-on. My eyes are closed. The curved silhouette of the sculpture rises in the background behind our heads, like a hook we are both hanging off.

She didn't post it, though, and I wonder if it still exists. I wonder if it ever did.

There's one of Liz and Bryan embracing at the airport, a bouquet of lilies in the hand she has wrapped around his neck, the flowers hanging upside down across his back as though they are being dried to keep forever.

A photo album has a way of making everything seem a foregone conclusion.

1.

I didn't tell Liz she'd been fired. Saying things aloud made them true.

Putting the question of her work visa out of mind, I focused on finding a lease for Liz and me to sign, thinking I could substitute one official looking paper for another. I convinced myself that if we only found the right place, she'd stay.

The apartment hunt was new to Liz, and tedious. When she'd moved to New York, she'd found a roommate, not an apartment, just like here. That time it had been a friend of a friend, a girl named Tracy, a few years older than Liz and about to start grad school at NYU. Liz couldn't even remember what she was studying—English literature, perhaps, or archaeology—something useless and heavy with books. They barely saw each other, and even after a year of living together were still uncomfortable on the rare evenings when they were both in the apartment. Tracy spent her days in the library and slept many nights at her boyfriend's apartment. Liz kept waiting for them to bond over something, but they had nothing in common, and Liz had no idea how to fake it.

She'd looked at the apartment, of course. Hers was the larger of the two rooms, with windows facing the alley behind the three-story building. It was fine.

We walked away from apartment number five, which I'd determined had "bad flow."

"What exactly are you looking for?" Liz asked as we sat down at a café.

I didn't answer at first, and then after a few moments of silence I merely shook my head and laughed quietly. Liz raised her eyebrows, though, pushing for more, and so I whispered, "I want a place that feels like a home."

Liz nodded. For once she seemed to actually understand what I was saying to her, which is perhaps why she didn't—couldn't—allow me to continue to search hopelessly. "No empty apartment is going to feel like that."

I took it as a generosity, a suggestion that anywhere we lived together would be home. But that's not how she meant it.

We sipped our drinks and looked across the table at each other and I nodded almost imperceptibly. I should have clapped my hands together and declared my intention to rent the last place we looked at, or the first. I didn't, though.

Love is not a builder and she cannot be built.

We walked back to our apartment in silence. Halfway home, past the convenience store where we paid our bills, the McDonald's we had never once entered, I reached out and took Liz's hand.

We could've had our ending that day. Liz could've gone back to the apartment and pulled out her suitcases, any explanation unnecessary. I would've nodded and silently began helping her load her clothes into the two bags.

"I've seen a lot of listings for one bedrooms," I would say finally. "Places you could afford."

Liz would smile.

"You can stay here, you know, back in your old room, until you find a new place."

"I don't think that's such a good idea."

"Right. So where will you go?"

Liz would shrug just one shoulder, only slightly, would smile. "I'll be okay," she would answer, handing me her keys on the way out.

But that wasn't our ending.

We got back to our apartment and I collapsed on the couch. Liz sat in the chair opposite me, not speaking any of the things she might have made true.

"This is exhausting, I know," I groaned.

Liz did feel exhausted.

"We've got three more to look at tomorrow. I promise, promise-promise that we'll just take one. The best one of the three. I know you're right. Wherever we live, we'll turn it into a home."

"I'm meeting with Sam tomorrow," Liz blurted, as though this were the same thing as telling me she no longer wanted to live with me at all.

"Oh." And then, "Do you trust my judgment? I could go look at them first."

Liz didn't respond, and I rushed to continue. "I wouldn't sign anything without you, obviously. But I could narrow it down. I'll look at all three, choose the best. We can go back together and look at it, and if you like it then we'll take it."

"Okay," Liz answered, because she didn't know how to say anything else.

When Bryan asked her to marry him, did she just say "okay?" Did she show up at the altar because she hadn't worked out an escape? I hope not.

2.

My last night with Liz, I lay in bed beside her, unable to sleep though my eyes ached for it. I was searching my memory for the moment things had fallen apart between us. It wasn't just one moment, but rather a series of them, a kind of slow crumbling away, like beach erosion. It was always like that. One or two grains of sand were carried away each day, and you either sat and watched not fathoming what you were losing, or, like me, you worked frantically, carrying new buckets of sand, to keep yourself standing on dry land. But where did all the new sand come from?

In the dark, my hand found her waist. "You're awake," I whispered.

She nodded in the dark.

My hand gripped her hip and pulled her closer, and then mouth found mouth and I kissed her, softly at first, and then more forcefully, wrapping my hand around her back as I did, pulling her even closer.

Another bucket of sand. Liz allowed herself to be

pulled toward me, allowed her t-shirt and shorts to be removed, clumsily but with no laughter, because it was dark and late and because we both seemed to want to believe that this was something we could do without any effort at all.

I stayed in my pajamas because Liz made no move to remove them. Instead she lay mostly still. My lips grazed her breast, almost incidentally, my fingers searched between her legs and found their way up inside her. I realized then, in the moment when I was working my finger in and out, that if I were a man this would all be different. I thought of Bryan, pushing his way inside of her, and then because it was dark and late, just holding himself still, his weight on top of her, pressing her into the bed, keeping her from floating away.

I waited for her to tell me to stop, to say "I'm sorry and this is all wrong after all," but instead, a soft moan rose from her throat. She moaned once then twice then a third time and then stopped and gasped for breath, once then twice, another moan and a hand gripped on my waist, and then my wrist, and a soft shudder and a muscle contraction and her hand pushed mine away and a soft sigh. I waited for her to thank me but she must've known that would be overdoing it. She closed her eyes and smiled just in case I could see her face.

"Good night," I whispered.

I imagined sand between my toes, more and more sand, covering my feet and then my legs. More and more sand, until someone finally just blew up the beach.

3.

Though she wasn't really meeting Sam, Liz walked to the Starbucks anyway. Where else would she go? She could've ducked down one of the side streets she passed, losing herself in the city. She could from here walk to Xiangyang Market, allow herself to be swallowed by the crowds of tourists, weaving their way up and down narrow rows between the open-air vendors. She could spend 20 minutes haggling via calculator for a knock-off purse that she didn't need, wouldn't buy no matter the price and then move on, waving and shrugging her shoulders to the baffled seller: good practice in disappointing people.

She never did turn off the main road, staying instead on the busy thoroughfare where car exhaust is a form of weather and the bodies pressing onward pull like the tides.

She wasn't meeting Sam but she was thinking of him, and ordered a Mocha Frappuccino in his honor. It was too cold a drink for the over-air-conditioned café, but she sat down with it anyway. She was wishing for a comforter to pull around her shoulders. She was wishing for home. She told herself that she wasn't avoiding me or our future; was instead avoiding her quicksand confusion. She would sit until she felt firm ground, and then she would come back.

In the meantime, she sorted through her mail, pulling out the messy pile I'd returned to her purse the night before. Three weeks' worth of staff meeting agendas; a stack of summer reading recommendations, organized by grade level, that should've been handed out to students; flyers advertising summer trips to Bali and Thailand and Tokyo, the distribution of which was paid for by various travel agents and tour groups. All over the city there were teachers at international schools looking through the trips with the same mild interest Liz showed them. In her mind there briefly existed a version of Liz touring Angkor Wat, snapping pictures of the monks in their saffron robes.

There was only one piece of paper with her name on it. Had Liz found the official termination document first, as I had, she might have been too distracted to notice the follow-up protocols for leaving her position, as I was. If I'd seen it, I would've taken it too.

Liz studied the list of dates, learning when her keys were due back to the office, when her work visa would expire. Thanks to the enigmatic green envelopes she'd been receiving all year, she wasn't surprised to be fired in such an oblique way. She exhaled deeply, seeing things as they really were.

Starbucks was overpriced and overcrowded, a place where people paid for the illusion of international sophistication, where they called their frothy, sweet drinks coffee, as though the word any longer held meaning. It was no different than any other place: everywhere people paid for their illusions, for the opportunity to name and rename the meaningless world around them. She needed to get out.

Sometimes a lie becomes the truth. On her way out of the Starbucks, Liz ran into Sam. They both saw each other and only one of them thought about pretending otherwise. Sometimes I think it was Liz. Other times Sam.

The one who wasn't pretending said hello, the other nodded in return, eyes cast down to the floor. There was a moment that would've been silence had they been standing anywhere but where they were.

"I owe you an apology."

Acknowledging a debt is not the same as paying it.

"I wasn't thinking about how that must have looked to your friends, and to you. I wasn't thinking about your feelings."

It wasn't a real apology, but Sam thanked her anyway because it was easier. "How are you?" he asked.

"I'm okay," she lied. "Do you want to sit down? Do you have time?" The repulsion she'd felt to the Starbucks disappeared as quickly as it had hit her.

She should've asked him to help her find a new job. After Sam nodded and ordered his coffee, after they'd found a spot in the corner to sit, Liz asked instead his advice on the problem he was least equipped to solve.

"If you don't love her, you should just tell her. You should just leave." He sounded confused that this was even a question. "You're free to do whatever you want." He sounded like he held it against her.

She saw the levels on which that was true. But still. How did she know what she wanted? Sam wouldn't be able to tell her. She asked him instead about his job, realizing that she knew so little about his life that it was the only thing she could think to talk about.

The conversation felt as awkward as their first session, except without any of the hope.

"Remember when you tried to teach me tones, and I just kept asking about spelling?" She laughed because once you've turned someone into a memory you can do that.

"I owe you an apology, too." Sam's answer that wasn't an answer.

"What do you mean?"

"I don't think I ever really wanted a language partner."

"What do you mean?"

He shrugged in a way he'd learned from Liz. "I just wanted a different kind of life."

"I know. We both did."

4.

Some stories get resolved.

Liz walked in the general direction of our apartment, imagining me at that moment assessing the closet space in a new master bedroom, mentally filling it with my clothes and hers. Then she hailed a cab and provided an address she'd heard me supply countless times before. Leaning back in her seat, she stared out the partially open window, then closed her eyes to the rush of air that greeted her as the car careened away from the curb. Her phone buzzed, a text from me:

The first two places were pretty good. I liked the second one best, but I have high hopes for the third place. I'll keep you posted!

Liz stared at the exclamation point, as though it were a clue to something. Then she put the phone back in her bag, empty now but for her wallet. She let out a sigh, loud enough that her cab driver turned around to stare at her. She scowled at him until he turned back toward the wheel.

"Just drive," she whispered.

Love shivers when the sun goes behind a cloud, and in the darkening evening, even in the month of May, she has goose flesh and a bone-chill that cannot be shaken. She cowers, looking for warmth.

She went to Blue Frog. During the day, the bar served just enough food to create the semblance of propriety for the people who came to drink. The glass doors that ran the length of the entrance were all folded open, allowing the early summer heat to creep in and creating the vague idea of a patio or beach, though the concrete that extended from the bar all the way out to the street in a seemingly unbroken line fought that notion. They needed bamboo floors, or a beach. Liz closed her eyes for a moment and imagined burying her toes in piles of cool sand.

She ordered a Bloody Mary, and then a second. They softened her edges, just as she'd hoped. She didn't care about the job right now—it was just a thing that she'd been given once, a thing that'd been taken away. It floated through her fingertips. The vodka so far was not enough to drown out the buzz of her phone, which lit up every few minutes with another message from me.

Apartment #3 is amazing! I'd written.

And then, I really think we should take it.

When can you be here to come look? I don't want to sign without you.

Okay, I'm assuming you're still chatting with Sam. Just text me as soon as you're on your way.

There's someone else coming in a couple of hours, so if we don't sign before then, we'll lose it.

She hadn't been keeping track of how much time elapsed between each text, and she pretended that she couldn't read the increasing panic in each message. If it were really an emergency, I'd call, she told herself as she ordered her third drink, even as she knew this depended on me having minutes on my phone, which was unlikely.

She shrugged, as though this were a debate she was

having with someone else. *I wouldn't answer anyway,* she mumbled to no one. Her phone lit up again as if in response.

On my way.

This was the message Liz had been waiting for, so she turned off her phone, slurped her drink, and waited for Dorian to arrive.

After Liz left Shanghai, I didn't see anyone out for a while. If I left my new apartment at all, it was only under duress, albeit the only one forcing me was me. I went to Chinese places that never made it into the text invites. I didn't go where the other expats went. I didn't see Dorian for months.

My mourning period ended eventually, and Dorian and I found ourselves at the same happy hours again. We would nod if we happened to make eye contact, but that was it. He was done with me, had gotten everything he wanted from his condo. And I'd never wanted anything from him.

But he wasn't done with me when he directed his cab to Blue Frog that day; it wasn't just that he wanted a front-row seat to our tragedy. He didn't really have time for day drinking. He had more unpacking to do, had to go buy dishes and pots and pans, towels and a new shower curtain. Having been held for so long in bureaucratic purgatory, Dorian was stunned by how quickly things had moved once he'd been released. He started sleeping in the new place, albeit on a mattress on the floor, just days after signing the papers. It was a new mattress. New sheets.

He'd been surprised, waking up that first morning, that he felt the same as he had the day before, and the day before that. He told himself that the transformation he'd been expecting to feel had actually begun many months ago; the apartment represented just the outward trappings of the change that was, really, nearly complete. He didn't notice it because he'd already grown accustomed to it.

He put the work of his new life out of mind as his cab pulled up. The bar was almost but not completely empty. Liz was the only one there sitting alone, the only one surrounded by three empty pint glasses, each of them containing ice in various stages of melt, straws, vegetable detritus.

"Those peppers are the best part," Dorian said as he approached.

Liz gestured toward the glasses, her hands surprisingly steady, her eyes clear. "Please. Help yourself."

He reached into the nearest glass and plucked out the canary pepper, snapping it from its stem in one bite. He didn't sit. He wasn't sure why.

"I'm going to go order some food," he said after a moment, and then turned and headed to the bar. He thought about asking Liz what she wanted, but knew she'd tell him she was fine, had already eaten, was too full of tomato juice. He ordered two hamburgers, fries, glasses of water and a beer for himself. When he got back to the table he cleared away the empty glasses before finally sitting down. He didn't understand where the urge to take care of her came from.

"What's going on?"

Liz raised her hands as though caught in the act of something, smiled. "I'm hiding out."

"Hiding?"

"Sasha went to look at more apartments this morning. She found one she really likes. She's waiting for me to come look so we can sign the lease."

Dorian nodded as though he understood something. "So how long do you think you'll have to wait here?"

"There's someone else coming to look at the place in a few hours. We'll lose it in then, I expect."

"Right. And then what?"

There was a long pause, during which perhaps they thought of me: sitting in a tea house somewhere, waiting for Liz, picking up my phone every other minute to check for a text, watching the clock on the wall and then fielding a call from the real estate broker, hearing her say she couldn't hold off, learning the apartment was gone; maybe they imagined me nodding and packing up my bag, paying for my tea and walking slowly back to the apartment I no longer wanted to wait for the girlfriend who no longer wanted me.

"Then I suppose she'll ask me to move out," Liz answered finally.

Dorian nodded. He did not ask the next obvious question—where will you go then?—because he didn't want to involve himself in solving that problem. Nor did he tell Liz what any rational, caring person might have said—that she was being cowardly and cruel, that I deserved better.

Their burgers arrived. Dorian drained his beer and ordered another.

"I'll have one too," Liz said before the waiter disappeared.

They began to eat in silence.

"I know what you're probably thinking," She said after she'd devoured half the burger.

"I doubt it."

"You're thinking this is a shitty thing to do."

"Yes, it's a shitty thing to do. That's hardly debatable. It's not what I was thinking, though. It's too obvious to even think about."

Liz laughed. "Okay. Fine. It's undeniably and obviously shitty. Then what were you thinking?"

"I was wondering how long Sasha will need to be single before she's ready for another relationship."

Liz put her burger down, took a long sip of beer before responding. "She's a fucking lesbian, Dorian. You're being delusional."

"Not really your problem, any more than you being shitty to her is mine."

It was true.

"Are you always so cavalier about everything?"

"Are you?"

Liz sighed and stood up. "Do you want another beer?"

Dorian nodded and Liz walked toward the bar on surprisingly steady legs. After a few minutes she returned to the table with his beer and a vodka cranberry for herself. "Okay, here's the thing: Homosexuality aside, Sasha doesn't even like you very much."

"What are you talking about."

"She thinks you're an entitled asshole."

"Thanks for the tip."

"I'm just trying to be honest with you."

"You want honesty?" Dorian was still smiling. "Sasha cheated on you. With me."

"What are you talking about?"

"Frank's going away party, at Zapata's? After you saw us kissing and stormed off. You think she went chasing after you? We fucked in a closet."

"How romantic."

Dorian shrugged. "I'm just being honest."

Liz stared down into her drink. She sighed loudly and Dorian knew he'd won something; he just wasn't sure what.

"So," she said, "here we are."

"Here we are."

Liz looked up at the clock on the far wall of the bar.

"I'm not going to freak out."

"Phew."

"I'm not going to get jealous and decide that I want to be with Sasha after all, just to spite you."

"That's a relief."

"Maybe you two would be perfect together."

Dorian searched for any sarcasm in the comment. He didn't know what to do with sincerity, and so he shrugged. "Maybe."

They drank.

I can guess now the story Dorian must have been telling himself. In his version, Liz finally turned on her phone to reveal a string of text messages from me, each one angrier than the last, until the final *Fuck you. We're done.* Liz would show it to Dorian and shrug; Dorian would smile. They'd finish their drinks and Liz would go home, preparing herself for whatever scene she'd face at the apartment. As soon as she was gone, Dorian would call me.

"I know what Liz did to you."

I would sob.

"She's been sitting in a bar for hours, waiting for you to lose the apartment, too afraid to just tell you the truth."

The sobbing would cease. Silence on the other line.

"She's on her way back now. I don't think you should be there when she arrives."

...

"I don't think you should be alone."

Dorian would provide his new address and though I would remain quiet he would know I was listening, that I would come. He pictured Liz arriving at the empty apartment, filled with all the apologies and half-truths she'd concocted in the cab on her way there, now with nowhere to lay them down.

Liz's story was different, though it started much the same, with the finality of text messages—the only kind of conversation that can't be undone. She would leave Dorian in the bar and would not think about him again. She would go back to the apartment where I would be pacing the living room, ready to break glass and shred a drawer full of Liz's clothes.

"I am sorry about how this happened, about the apartment, but let's just stop pretending, okay?" Liz would be calm. She would startle me into silence.

"I know about you and Dorian."

I would begin to cry.

"It's okay. I'm not angry. I think we've both felt for a while that things weren't right, that this wasn't going anywhere. Let's just agree on that and walk away now."

I would remain silent, and so Liz would repeat, for effect, "Let's just walk away."

Liz smiled and Dorian smiled and they both sipped their drinks and watched the clock, imagining text messages buzzing angrily across the city, nesting inside Liz's phone, gathering strength.

5.

Though I didn't hear from her at all that day, I signed the lease on the new apartment anyway. I thought I knew what I was doing. I signed and left, checking my phone after every step, still expecting her to message me at any moment. A few hours later, I called the realtor back. She was surprised to hear from me again so quickly, but once she learned that I hadn't changed my mind, she was happy to meet me downstairs in the lobby.

"I have to take some measurements," I told her, as if it mattered what I was doing there.

The place was stuffy, has remained so the entire time I've lived here. On the day I signed the lease, I spun in a circle, trying to project the kind of joy I knew I ought to feel. Then I stood alone in the middle of the empty apartment, unsure myself why I'd come. I sat down on the floor in the living room, leaning my back against the wall where one day soon I thought Liz and I would put a couch. I remembered the last time I moved into an unfurnished apartment: junior year of college, when my father had insisted I get out of the dorms, as though communal living had been the problem, as though depression was something you might catch on your way to the showers down the hall. My friends thought the place was "sweet," but to me it was just another prison. My first night there, when the apartment was mostly empty, my belongings still in boxes lined neatly against one wall, I'd done a thorough sweep for cameras—because I wouldn't put it past him—and having satisfied myself, retreated to the bathroom to throw up my dinner, my own private christening of the place.

Which explained why on that night last year I tasted vomit in the back of my throat. I swallowed hard and banished my father from that place.

Unfurnished was good. I wondered what Liz and I would choose together. I chuckled at the negotiations I knew we'd have: *Okay, you can buy that lamp, but then I want this coffee table.* I'd been in the old place since I arrived in Shanghai, and sometimes forgot that none of the furniture belonged to me. Liz and I eventually chose a new bedspread, and replaced the shower curtain, but nothing else was mine. For the first year I made a lot of jokes: about the hotel-quality paintings hung in gold frames with their gold oblong spotlights; the glass-topped coffee table with faux-coral base. "Oh, that's not so bad," people would say, until they got close enough to look down on the glass top and see the many marble fish living inside. They'd laugh and I would laugh and make drinks, and it was funny because we were all in the same situation, all of us unpacking our grimy suitcases amidst Chinese notions of luxury. But none of them stayed for very long, which was what made the joke.

I imagined a more understated décor: a sofa without tassels or fringe, a coffee table without an ecosystem. In my mind I saw the space, devoid of any knick-knacks, decorative vases, plastic flowers, with room for Liz and me to grow.

We had a lot to talk about. I knew that; I wasn't delusional. But then I thought I knew how the conversation would go. I heard it in my head: *the "I'm sorry," and the "I know, I understand, don't you see you're scared," the "we're in this together and I love you."* The conversation made me surprisingly happy to think about; I smiled and lay down on the floor. After a time, I remembered that the realtor was still downstairs waiting for me to finish the measurements, so I stood up and left the apartment.

"I've measured everything," I said loudly as I stepped off the elevator. "It's all going to fit."

The realtor looked confused but said nothing, and I smiled and handed back the key. In two days it would officially be ours.

6.

I could fill volumes with all the things I plan to say to people but never do. While Liz and Dorian were crafting their separate stories in their heads, I walked from our new apartment to a tea lounge down the street where I found a seat in the corner. My phone was on the table, but I didn't expect a message from Liz.

I ordered jasmine tea and thought about all the stories I'd never told Liz, that I'd convinced myself were immaterial. I thought I could fix it all on my own: the hurt and anger I felt toward my father that had been keeping me company for so many years; the growing heaviness I knew existed between Liz and me; the weight I'd been ignoring and that had frightened Liz away. I told myself I could erase it all.

Maybe Liz felt my determination, vibrating like a cell phone she couldn't turn off. Or maybe she knew the apartment had surely been signed hours ago. Dorian got up to go to the bathroom. He'd put the time out of mind or had had enough to drink that he'd forgotten what they were waiting for. Liz had never seen him so drunk before. Sitting there with him, though, watching it happen, she saw for the first time how funny he really was, and sad. She wanted to reach across the table and hold his hand, but instead she ordered another drink along with him, realizing that both gestures could be equally meaningful. At one point he looked as though he was going to kiss her. I knew the look. Liz smiled and knew immediately that she wouldn't turn him down. But he hadn't done it and now he was in the bathroom and Liz was staring down at her phone, about to turn it back on.

The screen lit up and for a moment that was all. It was just a glowing piece of plastic with nothing to tell her. Then it began to vibrate, over and over again as it registered the backlog of text messages that had been waiting, hovering somewhere in the air around the bar. She waited until the vibrations stopped before picking it up. Scrolling through the messages felt like eavesdropping.

I'm not sure where you are, but I'm trying not to get worried.

Okay, now I am worried, but I'm sure you're okay.

The other couple is pretty sure they want the apartment, but they're taking an hour to think. We need to swoop.

I'm going to meet the real estate agent. I think I understand what's going on here.

I signed the lease. I know you're probably hiding out somewhere. I'm not sure if you're reading your messages or not. I just want you to know that it's okay. I'm not mad at you. I understand. I know that you are nervous or scared and that this is a very big step for us. I know that deep down you want to do this with me, but that something's holding you back. It's okay.

Just come home and we can talk about it.
We have a new apartment!
Just come home.

I was ready to forgive anything, so sure that she was simply failing to be the person she most wanted to be. It never occurred to me that her intentions and her actions were the same.

Liz read the messages once and then again, trying to understand what they were telling her. Dorian returned from the bathroom and she passed the phone silently across the table. He read them more than once, too.

"Well," he said finally. "That's surprising." He looked at Liz, tipping his head to one side, trying to determine what it was about her that would inspire this kind of blind love.

"It is," she agreed. She couldn't tell if the feeling in her stomach was happiness or dread or just all the alcohol. For a moment she must have imagined the rest of her life, tethered to me through the strength of my denial, my determination.

"We need martinis," Dorian declared.

Liz did not disagree.

7.

At 10:30 that night, I turned off my phone. I unplugged the digital clock in our room, drew the curtains, and said a silent goodnight to the flashes of neon that had been dancing on the ceiling. I lay down on the bed and closed my eyes—though I wasn't tired—trying to remember back to a time when Shanghai surprised me. In my mind, though, it had always been the way it was on that night. It was people and light and noise and more people, and oh, the noise—car horns and jack hammers and welding tools, firecrackers and mopeds and traffic whistles—and always, everywhere you looked, more people: standing three rows deep at crosswalks, crowding the narrow entryways into supermarkets, pressing onto busses and trains and surging along sidewalks. In those crowds I'd wanted to disappear. And I had.

It happened instantly, at least in my memory:

I found a taxi and went to my hotel. It was really very nice. I realized on that first night without Liz that the worst thing about running away was that there was no one there to marvel at what I'd been capable of.

I vowed to tell her that: even in a city of 14 million people, even when you feel the weight of so many stares as you walk down the street, even when strangers stop you and ask to take your picture simply because of your white face, there's no one who notices what you are doing. I went to sleep thinking that I still had things to tell Liz—whole volumes of stories that were actually true—and it made me feel better.

While I slept, Liz drank. She didn't know what to say to Dorian.

"Why don't you just go back there instead of me?" she joked at one point, but then she saw that he was seriously considering it, weighing the potential of such a bold move, and she felt sad for him. You don't want to be Sasha's boyfriend, she must have wanted to say, but knew she couldn't explain herself. So she stopped trying to talk about me and instead got drunk enough that other conversation seemed possible.

"You own a condo."

"I do."

"In Shanghai. You own a condo in Shanghai. That's crazy."

Dorian shrugged. "Not that crazy."

"Have you told your mother?"

"Not yet," he answered. "I want to get it all set up and then send her pictures." Liz nodded in agreement as though it was his choice of a sofa and not his decision to settle permanently halfway across the world that would matter to his mother.

"Was it a hard thing to do? Buying, I mean?"

Dorian laughed. "You heard what I had to go through. All the forms. The silent 'partner' they gave me."

"Right. Yeah. I guess I mean, though, was it hard to decide to do it? To commit to something so permanent?"

"Oh, I don't know. It's kind of weird, but it wasn't really one moment that I decided to do it. There was the moment I guess that I decided to look into it, but that wasn't hard because I was only investigating. You know? Feeling out the possibilities. And then the wheels just started turning. It was just, submit this form, go here and stand in this line, that kind of thing. I just went through the process as it was laid out, and then I had a condo."

They both paused to think about this. Liz wouldn't have pointed out the obvious connection, because she didn't want to start talking about me again, but there it was: there was no moment when she officially decided that she'd be with me forever. She was only just investigating, and now here we were with a new apartment. A one-year lease would become two, would become four and suddenly we'd be 30-something, still going out every weekend, because that's what the 30-somethings did in Shanghai—Liz had seen them—still spending their money on travel and expensive restaurants, the kinds of things that proved their lives were forever transitory and therefore exciting.

"It's just like anything else," Dorian continued. "You just start the process without thinking too much about it, and before you know it, you've arrived somewhere you never thought you'd be."

"Before you know it," Liz echoed.

Dorian smiled and Liz waited for him to offer her more important life advice. Maybe he'd already given all he had though. She was on cosmo number four and couldn't quite be sure. Instead of advice, he reached across the table and offered the tip of his index finger, tapping softly against hers.

It was a kind of Morse code neither one of them could quite translate. Still they sat, finishing their drinks without making eye contact, allowing their fingertips to speak to each other through the drunken haze of disappointment in which they both felt trapped.

"Do you want to get out of here?"

"Yes," Liz answered quickly, suddenly feeling like she'd spent her entire life in that bar.

When they stepped out onto the sidewalk it was dark out. Liz couldn't remember when that had happened. She felt unsteady on her feet and caught herself on Dorian's arm. He put a hand on her waist. Before you know it, she thought, and then wondered how much of life was like this: a thing you said out loud first and then made come true.

What happens next is hazy. There was a moment when she was aware of the span of his hand on the small of her back. When he reached to unlock the door, she wanted to put the keys aside and press her palm to his, to feel her smallness in the bend of his fingertips.

There was hesitation, and then there wasn't.

"We don't have to," somebody said.

"But we should." Someone else.

She'd have to tip her head up, not down, to kiss him.

Love is not of the body. People remind themselves of this all the time, they do. They remind themselves and they forget; over and over again they forget. Love is not of the body and can only be found there if she is carried.

There are scenes that don't make it into my version of the story or hers, because I can't bring myself to conjure them and Liz certainly didn't photograph them.

8.

I woke up early, my hand reaching out in the dark searching the cool tangle of sheets on the other side of the bed for Liz, failing to understand why I found nothing. Maybe I lay there for hours, maybe not so long—the clock was still unplugged, my phone still off—but eventually I remembered. I stood up and walked to the windows, opened the curtains just slightly, allowing the hazy morning light to creep in. With it came an array of facts, marching into the room and lining up in front of the bed. Liz didn't come home last night. Liz went to a language exchange yesterday and didn't come back. Liz didn't respond to any of my messages. Liz didn't come see the new apartment. For facts, they told me very little. Nothing, actually. I had to get out of the apartment.

When I started walking, I didn't know where I was going. I certainly wasn't looking for Liz; even I knew that would be foolish. There was a part of me that was nervous about leaving, wondering what would happen if she returned to the apartment while I was gone. I wondered if I should have left a note: *You were gone, now I am gone, and soon we will both return and put behind us this idea of ever being gone again.* Or just, *Fuck You.* I wanted to be forgiving and beautiful and angry all at the same time, unsure as I was what she was really looking for.

Without meaning to, I walked to the closest Starbucks. How interesting, I thought as I found myself standing in front of the door, and then like a detective I stepped inside, aware it was the last place I knew Liz had gone. But remember, this is a love story, not a mystery. Liz hadn't been dragged out of the establishment, her body had not been dumped in an alley. She was just hiding, but then maybe she always had been.

There was no line; 8:30 a.m. was not a time the Chinese thought appropriate for coffee. I didn't really want any either, but I thought ordering something would bring me closer to her, as though I could channel my lover through hot espresso and foam. I tried to order my latte in Chinese, but the boy behind the counter looked at me strangely, and I accepted that nothing that day was as it seemed.

"A medium latte, please," I said, knowing I wasn't using proper Starbucks terminology. This, the boy didn't seem to mind. He handed me a mug and I winced, as though the sight of it physically pained me. Then I turned and found a seat in the corner, an armchair with a small end table beside it. Before I sat down I shifted it, ever so slightly to the left and toward the wall. After I sat, I found that I could continue to rotate the seat, little by little. Sip, sip, shift. Sip, sip, shift. By the time I was a third of the way done with the drink I was facing the wall, my back to the door of the café. I slouched all the way down in the chair, held my mug between my thighs.

One day I thought this would all be funny. I imagined us, telling and retelling the stories: *Remember when you disappeared for 24 hours?* Chuckle chuckle. *I sent you all those text messages, and you just ignored them. Oh, I know,* and I was sitting there wondering why you wouldn't just leave me alone. Oh, God, and I went to Starbucks. That's how desperate I was. Laugh laugh sigh. That's how alone I was. Hilarious.

I don't know how long I sat there: long enough to drink half a latte, to let the remaining half grow cold. I knew I needed to get a handle on time, could not let it keep slipping away unobserved like this. I needed to get home. The feeling seized me suddenly and I rushed out of the coffee shop, leaving my armchair facing the wall. I hurried down the sidewalk, contemplated hailing a cab but decided that given the traffic it might actually be slower than walking. Liz was on her way home, perhaps already in the apartment waiting for me—how else to explain the desperate and inexplicable urge I felt to get back?

I hopped up and down in the lobby of the building, trying to speed the elevator along with my mind. When I finally reached the apartment though, it was empty, just the way I'd left it. I sat down on the couch and cried, for five minutes, then 10, then 20, refusing to let time pass unnoticed any longer, even in my grief. After 25 minutes the tears dried up, and I understood that there was nothing left.

"Okay, Liz, I get it," I said aloud, as though we'd been having a conversation over the past 24 hours. We had, really: I had said the things I thought were right to say, I'd feigned that everything was normal through a fitful night of sleep, I'd tried to conjure a lost connection to her. Liz's response was the same after each of these attempts, and so I finally understood that there was nothing left for me to say.

I was still moving out of the apartment in three days. Nothing Liz had done would change the lease upon which I had signed my name. I went into our room to start packing. But when I opened the drawers, I was faced with Liz's clothes—her t-shirts and jeans and her old bras that I hated but also loved. I gathered it all in a ball—not everything she owned but enough—and carried it out to the small balcony off our room. I stood there for a moment, holding the bundle of clothes aloft, looking down at the driveway below.

That's when I saw her: the small figure walking in circles in front of the building, stopping and starting, sitting down and standing back up again. I held my breath, watching Liz walk to the end of the driveway, then turn around and come back. Finally, she walked close enough to the building that she was out of view. She didn't return, and I understood that she had come inside.

I stood frozen for a moment, still holding her clothes, unsure what to do with them. After a moment's hesitation, I peeled one bra out of the pile and let it go, watching as it fluttered down to the pavement below. I needed to see what it looked like when it landed. Then I stepped back inside to wait for Liz.

Love sat in the corner, squinting in the morning sunshine that streamed through the open curtain. She blinked slowly and saw shimmering dust motes dancing in front of her eyes. She held her breath and felt her pulse in her solar plexus. Exhaled. Held her breath again.

9.

There must've been a part of her that contemplated leaving without ever coming back to the apartment. Her clothes were replaceable, and wouldn't it have been nice to have a fresh start. But then she remembered the piles of cash in the locked drawer and she spoke the address to the cab driver more loudly than she'd meant to. She probably didn't understand any of this: her sudden need to flee from me, the pressure she felt, the slow sinking sensation. Her taxi crept through a tangle of Shanghai traffic while Liz tried to convince herself to feel something different. I can hear her thoughts in my head:

It's just a new apartment, she told herself first. *It's not really changing anything.*

Sasha loves you. She will continue to love you.

You'll find a new job.

You don't know what you want, what will make you happy, so how can you determine what is making you unhappy?

She loves you.

Sasha loves you.

Even as the refrain echoed through her head, she must have wondered if it was still true. I had loved her, before she disappeared for over 24 hours, before she refused to participate in our future, before she slept with Dorian. The cab pulled into the driveway and Liz realized that she'd wasted the entire ride on thoughts that would have been more useful to her yesterday. Today, all of her decisions had been made. The only thing left for her was to determine what to say to me when she went upstairs.

I'm just here for my money.
I'm sorry and I love you.
I'm sorry but I love you.
I know you slept with Dorian. We're even now.
I love you, but I'm sorry.
I have to go.

She paced in the driveway. She sat down on the curb just in front of the door, then stood up again. She conjured hour-long conversations with me in which she herself said everything she'd always wanted to say and then forgot the words instantly. She cried for a moment and then stopped, feeling stupid and naked but still not ready to go inside. She pouted briefly and called herself an idiot. She thought of blaming me, of blaming Dorian, blaming Bryan, or blaming her parents and then she forgot the meaning of blame altogether, failed to see what good it would do her and dropped it in the bushes. She walked halfway down the driveway, determined to go sit in a Starbucks for the rest of the day, until her absence would speak louder than anything she could say, and then she turned around, realizing that had already happened. Finally, she came inside.

She didn't know what she would say, but she decided, as she pressed the button for the twentieth floor and ascended toward the apartment that was once hers but now wasn't, that it didn't really matter. There were only four words—I slept with Dorian—that were important; Liz held them in her mouth like a jawbreaker. She would wait for the moment to spit them out and it would be done.

She opened the door to the apartment and was surprised to see me sitting at the dining table just a few feet away, staring at her.

"Hi," I said. Just like that. Liz must have thought of the days, months and months and months ago, before she knew the taste of me, the exact slope of my collarbone, when I was forever cooking and watching her. Should she have known something then? Did she know anything now?

"Hi," she answered.

"Do you want to sit?"

I know that she very much did not want to sit.

But I wanted for us to trade our stories: *Once upon a time, there was you and there was me. You thought that I was magic. We kept secrets from the world, and also from each other. We lied to everyone we saw. But lying was hard and soon we were just doing it to each other, and ourselves. Maybe I believed we could build a whole life like this, until you tried to run away. You looked back once to say goodbye, even though you didn't want to.*

"I'm not going to yell at you, Liz," I said. "Just sit down."

She sat. "Sorry." This could mean any number of things.

"I signed the lease."

"I know."

"It's a really nice apartment."

"I'm happy for you." I'm sure this was absolutely true.

I paused for a moment, considering my next words carefully. "Why aren't you happy for us?"

"I slept with Dorian."

I nodded slowly. "Is this a cause or an effect, do you think?"

I'm still thinking of the story: *I thought we could build a whole life like this, and so you slept with Dorian, trying to run away. Or: I thought we could build a whole life like this. Meanwhile, you slept with Dorian, and so you had to run away.* Either one worked.

Liz wasn't prepared for this question.

"I know you slept with him, too." It was neither cause nor effect: just another lie we told each other.

For the first time since Liz entered the apartment, I was surprised. I stood up from the table, laughing. "He told you that?" More laughter, and Liz must've realized she'd been stupid.

I walked away from the dining table, laughing and shaking my head all the way into the bedroom. Liz didn't follow. She'd told her four-word story.

10.

I sat down on the bed, looked over at the clock and saw a blank face staring back at me. I'd never plugged it back in. Minutes were important though, very important; I needed a way to gather them up and hold onto them forever. The inventor of the hourglass must have felt the same way, must have leapt for joy at the idea that time could be counted like grains of sand, could be contained within smooth glass and turned over and over within one's hand. He must've been giddy with that power.

I didn't know how many minutes passed. I didn't cry, which was surprising. Or maybe not. After some minutes had passed, let's say I heard the bedroom door click open and then shut. Let's say Liz sat down beside me.

"I thought we were more than this," I said.

"Sometimes we were," Liz answered.

"I thought we could handle anything."

"Why?"

"Doesn't everyone believe that? We can do anything together—isn't that what everyone says?"

"Most people are wrong. Divorce rates and all that."

"Oh. Right." I didn't tend to think about divorce in terms of percentages.

We sat in silence for five, maybe six grains of sand.

"So how can you ever tell?"

"Tell what?"

"How can you tell when to stay and fight it out? Things get hard sometimes, and people stay and fight. All the time it happens. Everyday people wake up and look at each other sadly. They yell and scream and cry and fuck and wake up the next day and everything's okay. Or maybe not the next day. Maybe it's a whole year of waking up and looking sad and feeling scared but deciding to stay."

"That's true." Liz nodded. "Some people maybe do that for their whole lives."

"It wouldn't take us that long," I whispered.

"It might."

"But it might not!"

"You can't force it like that."

"Force what?"

"The yelling and screaming and crying and fucking and waking up tomorrow. It doesn't work like that."

I looked down at my hands. "How does it work?"

"We say goodbye."

"I still don't understand why."

"This whole thing was a lie."

"If I were a man?"

"It would still be a lie."

"It was true for me, though."

"Okay."

I inhaled then exhaled. Inhaled then exhaled. Inhaled and stopped. Waited. Waited. Exhaled. Because the bed beside me was empty. It's impossible to say whether the conversation happened in my mind on that day, or for the first time right now, or maybe on a thousand days in between then and now.

When I went back out into the living room that morning, finally ready to talk, Liz was gone.

I stood there, looking at the air where she used to be. It was cool in the apartment and I shivered. I sat back down at the table and noticed the note. She had written on the back of an envelope, and so at first I mistook the paper for just another scrap of our lives, one more thing I'd have to deal with when I moved out. When I read it I laughed.

I got fired.

It was so easy for her to reveal her secrets; her stories were all so mundane.

11.

The next day I went out for tea. When I came back, I saw her keys on the table and felt a static electricity in the air that suggested I wasn't alone. I hurried through the apartment, looking behind doors, in the shower, under the covers, as though Liz and I were simply playing an elaborate game of hide and seek. The apartment was empty. After checking twice, I understood that I had misread the signs.

There was no electricity—just the disturbed dust motes swirling in the air, looking for a new place to settle. Liz's money was gone, along with her suitcase and her clothes. It was a coincidence, maybe, a twist of fate that we missed each other. She waited as long as she could for me to return, but then she had to catch her plane. Or, she'd been waiting outside the building for me to leave, so she could come back and pack up as quickly as possible before I returned. She hadn't looked for her necklace, which told me how little time she had.

I picked up the keys, feeling their weight, wanting very

much for them to mean something. But they were just keys. I had packing of my own to do.

There is no picture of Bryan's face as he follows Liz to baggage claim, as he realizes she is a completely different person, though he couldn't have explained exactly how.

There is no picture of the mark I left on her.

There is no picture of the day she unpacked and realized she didn't have her necklace. Did she regret its loss or was she relieved? I want to see the picture of her opening a box containing its replacement. A picture of the moment she decides against asking me to mail her the original.

This story isn't real, I tell myself. And then: *Close the computer.*

But I don't listen to myself.

Heather lives in Washington, D.C. She's a staffer on Capitol Hill and so her profile shows me nothing beyond the fact that she exists, that she has brown eyes and auburn curls and has once stood on a mountain overlooking a lake and smiled for a picture. Elsewhere on the internet, in photos beyond her control, she wears a black cocktail dress, at a wedding perhaps or a conference. The photo should—but doesn't—reveal which. And she is in a canoe at her college reunion. I assume from their smiles, and the fact that her companion is identified with a name but not a year of graduation that she is Heather's date and not a classmate. She's a pretty woman named Blair and when I find her on social media I learn she teaches preschool. I see her and Heather smiling in a kitchen.

Alice has a friend who baked her a cake when she passed the USMLE Step 1 after her second year of med school. She has a cat named Irma and makes inside jokes: about dating in LA, about anatomy and physiology, about a roommate she never names. She looks boring and happy and I miss the subtle jasmine smell of her.

I tell myself to go now to the airport and have a drink before my flight. *Have two.*

My father is not on social media, but my stepmother is. My 16-year-old half-brother is. There are stories and stories and stories, none of them meant for me to see. But I look through all of them anyway.

Still I don't forget about my flight.

Love waits until sunset, when the neon lights blink on, one at a time. They are the restaurants and bars, the shopping malls like beehives, the movie theaters; they are the skyscrapers full of condos owned by *lǎowài*, lining the river and stretching up toward space, pulsing, about to lift off; they are the hotels and the old banks, the tile-coated old apartment buildings, the guardrails along the veins of the city; they are the trees.

Love cranes her neck, looking up and up and up, searching for the dark. She wishes for stars. She says goodbye to Shanghai.

Acknowledgements

Before this book came the belief that I could be a writer. Thank you, Christopher Dollas, Mercy Carbonell, Ralph Sneeden, Karen Rile, Al Filreis, Paul Hendrickson.

Before that, the belief that a writer is a thing worth being. Thank you for that, Mom and Dad, and for the support you've each given me to pursue this dream.

I'm grateful to the many people who helped shape my writing and this novel: Brett Hool, Chris Khun, Dan Bevacqua, Eric Barkin, Frank Winslow, Heidi Julavits, Jamie Yourdon, Jason Pribilsky, Joanna Rakoff, Jonathan Dee, Jordan Foster, Kristin Walrod, Lidia Yuknavitch, Ramon Isao, Tye Pemberton.

Jaime Manrique: thank you for the questions you taught me to ask about my characters. Tahneer Oksman: thank you for being *Besotted*'s first, most patient reader, and for teaching me what critique should look like.

Annelisa Smith, April Custer, Emily Schoonmaker, Kathryn Moakley, Kendra Noyes Miller, Kimberly Kay, Kristen Boyd, Mary Milstead, Meghan Moran, Rachel Melissa, and Sarah Winter Whelan: thank you for teaching me to be a better reader. Thank you, Rachel Jagoda Brunette: the ways you keep me sane are too numerous to list.

Thank you, Leland Cheuk for believing in this novel enough to publish it, and Gigi Little for dressing it so perfectly to meet the world.

Kimberly King Parsons: thank you for being a trusted reader, a voice of reason, and the loudest cheerleader I've ever had. Tracy Manaster: for your masterful edits, motivational techniques, insights, honesty, culinary skills, and excellent taste in bars, I am eternally grateful.

To Jesse, for what you've taught me about empathy;
To Nikki, for more than 20 years of friendship, and for always believing in me even when I don't;
To Kate, for continuing on as my longest-serving editor, and for tricking me into moving to China:
Thank you. Thank you. Thank you.

About the Author

Melissa Duclos received her MFA in creative writing from Columbia University, where she was awarded the Guston Fellowship. Her work has been published in *The Washington Post, Salon, Bustle, McSweeney's Internet Tendency,* and *Electric Literature* among other venues. She lives with her two children in Portland, Oregon, and is the founder of *Magnify: Small Presses, Bigger,* a monthly newsletter celebrating small press books.

**7.13
BOOKS**

CPSIA information can be obtained
at www.ICGtesting.com
Printed in the USA
LVHW092333210719
624814LV00001B/176/P